Last Way West

a novel

Benjamin L. Owen

Author's note:
The writing style in *Last Way West* varies from textbook american punctuation in two noticeable ways. First, I use an extra carriage return instead of indenting to separate paragraphs. Second, I usually don't capitalize so-called proper nouns, such as *texas* and *honda*, except for individual names, or when writing outside the narrator's voice – like quoting a textbook or email. Thank you so much for reading. Sincerely, Benjamin L. Owen

ISBN: 1545075247
ISBN-13: 978-1545075241

To my best friends, you know who you are.

CONTENTS

CONTENTS...

The whole theory of the universe is directed unerringly to one single individual.
— Walt Whitman

Re-examine all you have been told... dismiss whatever insults your own soul.
— Walt Whitman

PROLOGUE
anamnesis

Learning is only a process of recollection.

– Plato

Excerpt from '*Wahenee: An Indian Girl's Story. Told by herself.*'

I am an old woman now. The buffaloes and black-tail deer are gone, and our Indian ways are almost gone. Sometimes I find it hard to believe that I ever lived them.

My little son grew up in the white man's school. He can read books, and he owns cattle and has a farm. He is a leader among our Hidatsa people, helping teach them to follow the white man's road.

He is kind to me. We no longer live in an earth lodge, but in a house with chimneys; and my son's wife cooks by a stove.

But for me, I cannot forget our old ways.

Often in summer I rise at daybreak and steal out to the corn fields; and as I hoe the corn I sing to it, as we did when I was young. No one cares for our corn songs now.

Sometimes in the evening I sit, looking out on the big Missouri. The sun sets, and dusk steals over the water. In the shadows I seem again to see our Indian village, with smoke curling upward from the earth lodges; and in the river's roar I hear the yells of the warriors, and the laughter of little children as of old. It is but an old woman's dream. Again I see but shadows and hear only the roar of the river; and tears come into my eyes.

Our Indian life, I know, is gone forever.

ZERO
juncture

If you turn the other cheek, you can be enslaved for a thousand years.
— Malcolm X

Walking home from school, Griffin Turner passed a crumbling building. Silver, slanted letters were spray-painted on the bricks:

RIP Isaiah

A poster tacked to a nearby telephone post said:

FOR RENT
SECTION 8 SPECIAL
New Tenants Receive Cash!!
Call Stan at
312-879-3049
Chicago Vista Investments

Griffin walked towards a long, semicircular granite bench. The blue-gray stone had words sculpted into it:

Everybody can be great because anybody can serve — Martin Luther King

An old man in an army-green canvas coat sat hunched over on the nearer end of the bench, his head almost in his lap, a white plastic bag full of stuff — maybe clothes — beside him.

At the other end of the long bench was a cluster of three young men. Griffin knew them well — everyone did. They controlled all the drugs moving in and out of the neighborhood. Within this world, they were kings, wise men who commanded respect.

Beside the first man, Gasp, was a thin roll of paper towels and a clear plastic cup half-full of golden liquid. Beside him, the second man, Melch, sat fiddling with small, semi-transparent sheets of blue plastic. The third man, Balty, had long dreadlocks and wore a white, sleeveless t-shirt that showed off his solid build. He had tattoos all over his body as well as most of his face, and his front teeth were completely covered in gold.

"What you know, Griff? Or what you need to know?" Balty asked.

Griffin stopped in front of the three men. "Nothin'. Just walkin' home from raby."

"Raby, baby, *maybe*. Well, I'm glad you're comin' home from school instead of never goin' at all – like me."

"Yeah," Griffin said. "Well, everyone needs some education to survive. Right?"

"*Education?*" Balty laughed. "My classroom was right here in the streets. How I started? I was born right here in chicago's west side, bullets flyin' over my head when I was a baby in the *crib,* and I've been doin' *nothin'* right since I was thirteen – smokin' dirty, drinkin'. As the years went on, things changed some – not *everythin'*, just some things. But the weed and coke smokin' – that ain't *never* gonna stop, straight up."

The men laughed.

Balty continued, "Now this stuff keep me calm and keep me from killin' people out here. Y'all need to *legalize* this." He held up a brown paper cigarette. "Hey Melch, tell Griff what happened last night."

Melch looked to be in his early twenties. A red baseball cap was perched sideways on his head. He wore a red winter vest and a silver chain with a crucifix. He said, "I ain't gonna lie to you – all last night, right? I'm coked up, I'm *peeped* up, I'm outta my mind. I got the graveyard shift, which is eight at night to four in the mornin', right? It's about two o'clock in the mornin', and I go up to the bathroom. Anyways, I'm sittin', I'm takin' me a couple toots. Next thing I know, I hear this *ruckus* right here."

Melch pointed at the bushes just past the bench. "Right there in that little area right there. And I'm sittin' down, peekin' out, tryin' to see what's goin' on. Anyway, I hear this man yell, 'Yeah, bro, that's *you!*' or somethin' like that. And next thing I know, I hear a dude say, 'Man, *please* don't kill me!' And that's when I look, and when I look, I seen the dude shoot like three times, *three or four times, man.* He killed the man – like point-blank range, sittin' *right here,* man! It's crazy. It went down right in front of me."

The skinny old man sitting alone at the other end of the bench rose up and looked at them with wide eyes, gripping a cane in his hand. He was fiftyish and wore a white t-shirt under a green army fatigue jacket. Pointing his cane at them, he said, "What you *gettin'* outta killin' a brother, huh? You ain't gettin' *paid.* It don't make no sense, man. These killins' are so sad man, but I just – I'm just prayin' that god sees me through one day at a time. Prayin' is what we gotta do, cause if we don't, we ain't gonna make it without *him.*"

The old man pointed at the sky with his cane. "That's where your help and your strength come from – the lord! – *mmm hmm.* The first verse I learn out the bible was the twenty-third psalm. 'The lord is my shepherd, I shall not want. He maketh me lie down in green pasture, he leadeth me beside the still waters. He restore my soul, he leadeth me on the path of righteousness for his name's sake. Yeah, though I walk through the valley of the shadow of death, I shall fear no evil. For god is with me.' That's the first verse I learned, the twenty-third psalm. Yeah man, I read my bible from *genesee* to revelation."

Balty laughed. "Really, Sam?"

The old man said, "I went to prison and caught three years for *shootin'* a dude's pants off."

Everyone laughed.

"I ain't lyin'. Be *snatchin'* my wallet. I done near three and I caught two more years after *that.* Brother tells me I can't lift on that bench. I said, 'You're an inmate like *me,* man!' And then he got up on the threesome and I waste him *all* up."

"No!" Balty said.

"I lift his head up *outta* there. Yeah, they sayin' *that* brother's Sam Gilly from the bible."

Everyone laughed. Balty said, "I appreciate you, Sam."

Gasp said, "I hear you, Sam." He turned to Griffin, handed him an envelope and said, "This goes to Mades." Then he handed him a brown paper bag. "Give this to your momma, Griff."

"Ok," Griffin said.

"You're special," Gasp said. "You're gonna do somethin', Griff. Keep goin' to raby. Get smart so you can save the rest of us, or at least yourself. Someone's got to do somethin'."

"Ok," Griffin said.

::<>::<>::<>::<>::<>::<>::<>::<>::<>::

Griffin pushed on the partially open apartment door and saw a semicircle of women, their backs toward him. The room was a haze of smoke. There was a half-empty gallon of no-brand gin on the crooked, wooden magazine table, an overflowing plastic ashtray, a rectangular cardboard container of orange juice, an assortment of lighters, matches, and red plastic cups.

"I've never known *who* the daddy is and I don't *care*. He wasn't much if I can't even remember. I'm not even sure what *night*! It might've been Aunt Kavina's wedding. I was *sooo* drunk, I don't even know. I mean, I don't remember doin' it!"

The women laughed.

"You're like Mary and the baby Jesus," said a different woman, and they laughed louder.

"Mom," Griffin said.

"What, Griff?" she asked, turning to look at him. "What? I'm busy."

"We have the meetin', mom. At school."

His mother took a drink from her red plastic cup. She took a puff off her cigarette, inhaled, held it, exhaled, then spoke. "I forgot. You should've reminded me. I'm in no shape to meet with no principal."

"It's the guidance counselor."

"Griff, I don't care if it's Obama and Cleopatra. I'm not goin' anywhere other than right here."

Griffin studied her. Mom was like the weather – always unreliable. He'd almost learned to accept that. But he'd reminded her of this meeting every day for a week, including this morning. The guidance counselor wanted to meet with both of them. Mister Nathan said maybe Griffin could get a full scholarship to the university of illinois. He wanted to talk about college – an impossibility that maybe could happen.

He'd hoped mom would be proud; instead, she was drunk at three in the afternoon.

"Here," Griffin said, handing her the brown paper bag. "Gasp said give this to you."

Mom opened the bag and took out a white envelope, some twenty-dollar bills, and a bundle of twisted cellophane. She looked inside the white envelope, then put everything back in the bag.

"It's not for forty minutes, mom. There's still time to get ready."

Mom glared at him with half-drunk anger in her eyes, but he also saw a glimpse of uneasiness. Buried inside her, part of her knew she was astray – so far astray that she had to act blind. If mom opened her mind enough to see that she was wrong in this moment, then she would have to see that she'd dismembered her entire life beyond repair. So it was best to stay oblivious, to stay within the fuzz of meaningless laughter, plastic cups of gin and juice, and clouds of menthol cigarette smoke.

"Nope. I got plans," mom said.

Griffin looked into her glazed eyes and realized there was no point in arguing. He was talking to gin and whatever was in the brown paper bag. There was no one else there.

He left.

::<>::<>::<>::<>::<>::<>::<>::<>::<>::

A few hours later, Griffin sat on a bench in garfield park, across the street from the roseland food & liquor store. On a yellow plastic sign, in red and blue painted letters were the words 'COLD BEER - SNACKS - POP - DAIRY - FULL LINE OF GROCERIES'. Six blocks away was raby, his high school, and his meeting with mister Nathan, the guidance counselor, was over.

Sometimes when he thought about college, it seemed a stupid waste of time. He'd never known anyone who went. What was there to learn that he hadn't already learned on the streets? Life was hustling, fighting, insanity, mayhem, and death. School had nothing to do with reality.

But other times, college seemed like the only hope he had to hold onto. If he just stayed on the streets, passing cash and cellophane around, then he'd be Balty in a few years, king of a park bench, ruler over a dominion of sleaze. If he went to college, maybe he could leave all this lunacy behind.

The glass skyscrapers that soared above chicago were built by men who had used college educations to create and build. Balty's education, the academy of the hood, was good for quick cash, gunfire at four in the morning, and old ex-con alcoholics pointing canes at the sky, screaming about the bible.

A man shuffled up to him and spoke – the fourth person to ask him the same question in the past fifteen minutes.

"No. I don't know where to score," Griffin said.

He needed to inventory his options and make some choices. Mom didn't care, nobody else cared, so why did he care?

He didn't care, so much as he was tired: tired of being broke, tired of being surrounded by idiots – his idiot mom, idiot classmates, idiot teachers, idiot gangbangers, idiot mister Nathan who kept sitting him down and talking to him about his future. He kept asking a question that Griffin couldn't answer, "What are you gonna do?"

What am I gonna do? The future was drugs and gangs. There was the cops and brothers game, forever. That was the only game he'd ever seen played, and he could become the best who ever played it.

Mister Nathan told him, "Griffin, an education and hard work is the only way out of this crap. This life is crap – crappy project apartments, crappy people, crappy neighborhoods. But you gotta relax, Griffin. You gotta take your time. Nothing great will happen overnight; it's all a big slow, gradual unfolding that requires busting your butt for years. There's something special in you. You see more clearly than others. But you don't have anyone to help you use your gift, and because of that, you're going to make dumb choices that become permanent. You're eighteen in a few weeks. The next time they pick you up with dope in your socks and a gun in your jacket they'll get you for dealing and it will be adult time, felony time, and doors will slam closed on you quick. Your life will be over before it started."

"So what are you sayin'? Sit inside college, broke and bored to death for four years?"

"Yeah, I'm saying do the right thing, even when it's dull. A lot of times, doing the right thing is really monotonous. Get used to it. Listen, I could get you a full scholarship to the university of illinois. They want kids like you who come from places like this."

Griffin paused. He thought of the glass towers rising above the city. He thought of men in suits. He thought of Balty's gold teeth and tattooed face. "You think I could get a scholarship?"

"If you keep the same grades. If you study for the standardized tests. If you stick with baseball this spring. And if you *stop* dealing – get a job instead, at the arby's maybe. A lotta ifs. But you can do it."

Griffin smiled and laughed. "There's *no way* I'm workin' at arby's. That horsey sauce is toxic. I don't even wanna guess what's in it. I have a lot of theories about what that goop is."

Mister Nathan laughed. "Church's? McDonald's? Something other than the benches, Griffin. I'm telling you, I've seen it too many times to laugh about it. You'll get busted, and in an instant, your life will be over."

"Ok, I'm hearing you. I'll really think about it."

"*Think?* There's no time to think. There's kids whose parents are hovering over them right now while they practice their standardized tests, driving 'em to music lessons and calculus tutoring so they can polish their college resumes. That's who you're competing against! Life's a competition. The world doesn't care what color anyone is, or who was a slave two hundred years ago, or who deserves a break, or whose drunk mom raised seven babies in a two-bedroom apartment. The big lie is that there's anything fair in life. Nothing's fair – especially on the west side of chicago."

Griffin said, "Look, I don't believe life's fair. You don't need to worry about me havin' any false illusions. Last month, I didn't go home for a week and my mom never noticed. She's not here because she's too busy drinking out of her plastic cups, teeterin' in front of the stove, stirrin' up another batch of macaroni and margarine for the pile of kids in front of the television."

"Yeah," mister Nathan said. "We're saying the same thing. So let's do it, Griffin. You do it and I'll help you. Now, you have to get good scores on these standardized tests and that means you have to prep. The prep course costs three hundred bucks, ok? You come up with three hundred bucks and you'll whip that test and you'll get paid to go to college and you'll *do* something with your life."

::<>::<>::<>::<>::<>::<>::<>::<>::<>::

Walking up the stairs to his apartment, Griffin thought, *A college scholarship. It's really possible.* He was excited to tell his mom.

Inside the apartment, the women were gone and mom was in the kitchen, sitting at the plastic folding table with her eyes almost closed. In front of her was a plastic cup with a picture of the burger king on it. A cluster of kids sat in front of the television – he had five half brothers and half sisters and they all had friends who roamed in and out. Sometimes he had to look twice to know which of the assorted kids shared his blood.

Everyone was too drunk, on gin or television, to see that he had come in. Before anyone noticed he was there, he turned and left.

::<>::<>::<>::<>::<>::<>::<>::<>::<>::

Griffin walked over to the benches. Balty was there, amidst a group of people.

"What's *good?*" Balty asked.

"Everything," Griffin answered. Balty held out his hand, Griffin shook it, and took the bills from Balty's palm into his.

Standing amongst the group, distracted, Griffin heard just snippets of patter as people came and went, as faces appeared and faded. He couldn't piece together who was saying what to whom, or find any coherence in the stream of scattered talking.

"Six one thirteen," said a man wearing a white, long-sleeved sweatshirt.

"What's happenin'?" a new voice asked.

I'm wasting my time, wasting my time, wasting my time, Griffin thought.

A man said, "Yo, this is how we rock 'round here, man – five hundred a shoe, five hundred a shoe." Griffin looked and saw blue plastic shoes, gleaming in the lamplight.

A young woman said, "Yeah, I'm cute. Bills ain't even *paid*, but I got car notes on my weaves – that's how I do it. Bye! Comin' to a screen near you."

I'm wasting my time, wasting my time, wasting my time...

Someone said, "I been shot *all* up. I ain't got nothin'. I gotta get off the streets – it's crazy out here. There's no ways of winnin' and a *hella* lotta ways of losin'."

A man spoke, "Cause we all know, man, come from this motha, you eitha gonna *sell drugs*, or you gonna get you a bogus job payin' *twelve dollas* an hour, then you gonna *have* to go sell some drugs, know what I'm sayin'? Like this is all a *maze* to get you right back on the block sellin' drugs."

I'm wasting my life, wasting my life, wasting my life...

Griffin couldn't follow the point of the disjointed conversations. Nothing anyone said made sense. *This place is a prison,* Griffin thought. It's poverty, ignorance, and laziness combined to create a stew of madness that's contagious. *Insanity is contagious,* he thought.

Griffin heard mister Nathan speak to him from the dark. "You can go to college – all you need is three hundred bucks for the test prep. There's scholarships that pay for everything for brothers trying to get out of this. You got a real shot. Get the money so you can practice for this test."

Griffin stepped out on the street, happy but worried; excited but concerned. His next step was clear. Now he had one thought on his mind – getting the three hundred dollars.

Forget arby's. He'd talk to Balty, do just a few more runs, and then be done with all this forever.

Balty was the best way to make a quick roll of bills.

ONE
luceo

Life is a great sunrise.
– Vladimir Nabokov

Mark Halberstam sat on a bench near the end of a dock, looking out over a lake. A small boat was moored in the distance. A slight breeze rocked it. Waves rippled out from the craft, journeying softly toward him.

The clouds had touches of pink, purple, and blue on their fringes. Behind them was golden yellow light. He couldn't see the sun, but he knew it was rising because the entire landscape around him was turning golden blue. The slight breeze picked up just a bit, as if nature was trying to welcome the sun, to bring it forth into the morning.

This sunrise will always be here, he thought.

I'm pregnant. Gaia's words kept echoing through his mind, paralyzing him. He had done everything wrong. He was panicking inside, overwhelmed. He was going to be a father. Choices were disappearing. He looked back at his parents' house. A brown maple leaf scudded across the lawn. Twenty yards away, a chipmunk stood on its haunches.

When Gaia told him, he refused to believe. He dodged reality by splitting into two people. Sometimes, he was shell-shocked – a bewildered boy who couldn't look anyone in the eye. More often, he a was a partying idiot, going beyond the limits of excess into a fantasy world of blurred drunkenness, crazy one-night hookups, pointless consumption, and jaded cynicism. He was becoming addicted to short-term gratification, hooked on the thrill of satisfying his lust and greed, like a junky hooked on heroin. Despite all his best intentions, he kept giving in to every selfish impulse. Evil was becoming a habit, and if he wasn't careful, it would take over. There was a seed of depravity inside him, grasping to take root; he had to stop it from growing before it twisted his soul. He had to evolve to become a loving, caring father. He had to escape the lure of mindless hedonism before it consumed him beyond salvation.

He should be righteous. He should marry Gaia.

Another option was to leave – just run. Escape, put this behind him, start over somewhere else. As years went on, people would accept his retreat; they wouldn't forgive him, but they would get on with their lives. The sting of his betrayal would fade, and the people in his new life wouldn't know of his weakness. But wouldn't karma chase him down?

It was impossible to know how things would work out. He dreaded telling his parents – *his dad*. He was petrified of talking to her parents – *her dad*. What would those men think of him?

He tried to still his mind, to just focus on letting his senses absorb the sensations of the warm morning. The breeze had become firmer and steadier, taking only brief respites so the bending leaves could rest.

Could he marry Gaia? Could he promise to love her forever? There were parts of her he *could* love forever – her smile, her gentleness, her laughter, her simple understanding, her genuine enjoyment of life, her stubbornness. But there were also parts of her he could hate – her complacency, her stubbornness, her inexplicable moodiness when she just shut him out and ignored him for days at a time.

What *exactly* was love? Define it. How could anyone ever know if they could love someone forever? Every individual had flaws, and even if someone found the perfect match, people changed, so it was impossible to predict if love would endure. Every couple faced an unknown future. They could fall out of love. They could fall *more* in love. If Romeo and Juliet had stayed alive, their passion could have dimmed; Romeo would fume that Juliet was wasting toilet paper, she would nag Romeo about drinking too much, and both would be annoyed by the in-laws.

If he married Gaia, there was the possibility of happiness, the possibility of bitter divorce, or, infinitely worse, the possibility of a tortuous in-between – a muddling purgatory.

If he didn't marry her? He'd be a single father, observing his child's life from a distant orbit. He'd sit a couple rows behind Gaia, her inevitable future husband, and their children; he'd sit alone at sporting events and school concerts, and then he would leave and do what? Go out to eat alone? Go home alone and stare at screens? Travel through life with a new girlfriend every few months, living in a ghost world of permanently disposable relationships?

Do I ever plan to get married? Yes. Life is trivial enough. Without a family, it's even more pointless. So at some point, I want to be a husband and a father. And if that's going to happen, is now the time? Is Gaia the right woman?

Did the right woman exist? He needed to lower his standards if he was ever going to marry. Finding perfection was impossible, but how far down must he lower the bar? He was too quick to spot the smallest flaws — meekness, arrogance, inconsistency, a skin blemish — he'd never wholeheartedly admired anyone for more than a week. But if he ranked his admiration and respect for others, Gaia was at the top of the list, only behind some authors he'd never met. He would probably never meet a better woman.

I'll ask Gaia's dad for his blessing. I'll do it.

Mark looked up. Fresh touches of orange edged the clouds. The sun had risen; the entire landscape around him was ablaze with morning light.

A new day had begun.

TWO

harbinger

Study the past, if you would divine the future.

— Confucius

Selected from *THE NEW YORK MESSENGER* Article Archives
August, 2013

Feds Won't Block State Pot Legalization

BY JOSEPH BURSTIN

DENVER – In a decision with historic implications, the federal government announced that it will not stand in the way of marijuana legalization in Colorado or Washington state.

But it will be watching closely.

Deputy U.S. Attorney General James Cole said in a press release yesterday that the government won't block marijuana legalization in the two states. The federal government also will not close down recreational marijuana stores. However, if the two states can't keep marijuana from being trafficked into neighboring states, Cole said that the federal government would crack down.

President Barack Obama previously indicated that marijuana users would not be targets for prosecution. But Thursday's memo is the first time federal officials have offered explicit legal cover from federal prosecution. That means that marijuana businesses in Colorado and Washington will be able to operate without federal interference.

"Today's announcement shows that our meddling federal government is finally respecting the will of Colorado voters," Governor John Hickenlooper said in a statement.

States' rights advocates hailed the news as a huge victory in a larger movement. Madison Telvert, a libertarian activist in Colorado, said, "This is a historic step toward ending federal government interference in our local communities. We don't need the tyrannical feds. This sends a clear signal that states have the freedom to determine all their own laws."

Anti-marijuana groups expressed alarm. Fay Calvin, head of the group Save Our Society from All Drugs (SOSAD), said, "The American government has surrendered to the whims of bong smokers. There will now be a tsunami of young Americans living in marijuana slavery."

As lawmakers and regulators in both states craft rules for the recreational marijuana industry, the memo shows federal officials realize that some federal laws can no longer be enforced. "The federal government has limited resources to enforce these laws," Cole wrote.

Joseph Burstin can be reached at burstin@newyorkmessenger.com.

THREE
rarity

A family is a mystery.
– Sharon Olds

Happy anniversary, Gaia Halberstam thought. *Time flies.* She and Mark had been married sixteen years today. At times, it seemed like just yesterday she'd been a broke, unmarried girl with a baby on the way, trying to make the scariest decision of her life – Give her baby up? Abort it? Marry Mark? Move home? Run away and do it all on her own? Every choice was wrong, but she had to make one, so she'd married Mark. Now, in a slow flash, they'd been married sixteen years and had four kids. Julie, their oldest, would be applying to colleges in a year.

Sixteen years. Maybe things had worked out for the best. She and Mark still couldn't seem to get completely in sync, but they managed. *Does any couple ever have it all figured out?* Every relationship was a journey with twists and turns. And bumps. And steep hills. Many parts of life were good. Their four children were incredible; she couldn't imagine a world without them. Money was no problem now; a huge upgrade from their early years of living on shuffled credit cards. But in other, subtle, less measurable ways, things were somehow worse. Getting along with Mark was becoming more difficult. They'd been so immature when they married, and over time they'd become a different couple, only distantly related to the infatuated young lovers they'd once been. They'd been consumed with lust for each other. Now, she loved Mark, but they weren't connecting.

Gaia looked out the window. She loved being at their country house. It just felt more *normal* than their new york city penthouse or the oceanfront mansion. This place reminded her of growing up in her small indiana town. Through the open windows came the sounds of birds and a single car driving by – this place was different than manhattan in all the right ways, slower and more natural.

I could live here all the time, she thought. But that would take the kids away from their schools, their friends, and everything they were used to. Mark needed new york city; he wouldn't ever move. But he was hardly home anyway, always traveling for work, as he was today. After being with them for a miraculous four days in a row, he'd left this morning, going to niagara falls for business.

At her request, he'd sent all the household staff home for a few days. "I just want us and the kids to be normal," she said. "To do things for ourselves. Make our own food and our own beds. Do our own laundry. God forbid we stop waiting to be waited on. It's not great for the kids, Mark. They need to be with just us once in a while."

To Gaia's surprise, Mark, who usually automatically disagreed with her, said she was completely right. So when they arrived, there was no one there to bring in their bags. They made their own meals. The kids had a list of chores waiting for them each morning. Mark worked all across the property, repairing fence slats, landscaping, mowing the lawn; and she and the kids joined in, surprised at how much there was to do and how satisfying it was to do it.

Gaia lay down on her daughter Margaret's bed, positioning herself between sorted piles of laundry and losing herself in the patterns of dappled sunlight that were dancing on the white fabric window shades and the thin, sheer curtains in front of them. It was like artwork – a living, moving, abstract painting that calmed her, hypnotized her almost, making her drowsy. She had so much to do today, but she decided to take a break and just sit here. Now that Mark was gone, taking his unrelenting expectations with him, she could relax a bit with the pace of the housework.

It was seductive, the kaleidoscopic patterns and patches of sunlight shifting as the blinds and curtains swayed with the slight breeze that was coming in through the open windows. She felt the breeze softly comb through her long, softly curled, brown hair. She heard a distant train whistle and wondered when the last time was she'd heard that. There was a train somewhere around here, over near east road, but she couldn't remember the last time she'd heard it. She couldn't remember the last time she'd been so tired that she needed to sit down in the late morning to rest. The breeze and the patterns enticed her, reminding her of lying in bed after making love, feeling complacent and not wanting to move, so time could almost pause and her contentment would be slow to fade.

The next thing Gaia knew, she was waking up, confused about where she was and why she found herself waking up in the early afternoon, an experience she wasn't familiar with. She wondered what time it was. She picked up her phone and set the alarm on it for two, so she could relax and not worry about falling asleep again; the alarm would wake her up before the kids were supposed to be home from their hike.

Across the bed was one of Margaret's many notebooks. It had a white background with small, jagged blotches of black, forming a pattern. She opened it and saw that it was her daughter's writing journal; there were pages after pages of handwritten notes, poems, and journal entries. She heard a bird chirp outside.

Gaia stopped at the last entry in the notebook and read,

Sunday Breakfast: A Rarity
by Margaret Halberstam

It's simple enough, the
small bowls of raspberries beside
every plate like a kiss on the forehead
from my dad:

A surprise.

Golden glowing buzz of warm
gurgles from the radio in
the place where the microwave used to be.

There are things to do later,
chores to be done and
rooms to be cleaned.
Dishes to be washed and
yards to mow.
But for right now,
we are in the kitchen

and we are laughing.

Apprehension is the largest
component.

It's the waiting that is
exciting. The eggs are
ready but the sausage is
still frying, is the toast
ready yet?
We are pale pink
and yellow and soft
orange and we
are happy.

There isn't often time
for this anymore.
We are still a family but
we are older than we were.
When was the last time I
saw my mom smile like this?

Laughing with my dad like they
are in a picture hanging on the
fridge from when they
first met, sitting on a worn
couch with love and lust
in their eyes – exasperated
with whoever is taking their picture.

The food is finally ready,
and perhaps the smell
was better than the taste.

I realize I don't even like
breakfast food all too much.

But there is love here,
I am loved and we are
loved and if you
were there you
would be loved too.

When the plates empty
it is time to do dishes
and then it is time to
do chores and
clean rooms and

mow lawns.

And all day
throughout the chores
and the cleaning and
the mowing, the soft
warm gurgle of the
radio will hum quietly
in the background of
everything.

Happiness.

As Gaia finished reading the poem, a tear dripped from her cheek onto the page, another tear followed a small creek that ran down her neck towards the top of her breasts. Margaret's poem was perfect.

She closed the journal but she kept her hand on it, her fingertips touching the cover as she fell back to sleep.

FOUR
falls

We live in an age when unnecessary things are our only necessities.
— Oscar Wilde

Mark Halberstam sat in room six-twenty-eight of the marriott fallsview hotel, waiting for room service to deliver a bucket of beers and a glass of whiskey on the rocks. He looked out his window at niagara falls. Millions of gallons of water poured in from lake erie every second and then plunged over the cliffs. He saw a ferris wheel, a casino sign, and fireworks exploding upward in bursts of colored fire before falling from the sky. A rainbow of man-made lights rotated underneath the falls. All this touristy pizzazz struck him as surreal and — somehow very wrong.

Happy anniversary, Mark thought, watching the flood of water…fall…
                                                                                    …fall…
                                                                                        …fall…

He and Gaia had been married sixteen years today. *Time doesn't just fly; it moves faster than that. It teleports us forward into the future. Sixteen years ago, I was there. Now, I'm here.* It seemed like last week he'd been bewildered and lost, sitting on a park bench next to Gaia, feeling like he was in a nightmare while she told him she was pregnant with their baby, his daughter, Julie. He remembered the tense conversations, the arguments, the bewildered tears, and the realization that there was no answer that made any sense. Every option was fraught with uncertainty. But through it all, Gaia had been there for him, loving him, helping him see some path forward that gave them a shot together. Now, an instant later, they'd been married sixteen years and had four kids. Julie was driving, she'd be applying to college in a year, maybe she'd even get into a decent school if she'd just buckle down and really prepare for her standardized tests.

Sixteen years. A lot of things had worked themselves out. He wasn't on the same page as Gaia, but at least they were usually working from the same book. Their four children were miracles. Money was no problem now; being a billionaire was a huge upgrade from years of debt. But inside him, in places he let no one see, things were getting worse. Being a good person was becoming more difficult. He'd been self-centered when he'd gotten married, and over time he'd become more selfish, not less. He was becoming consumed with lust and greed. He loved Gaia and his family, but a part of him was disconnected from them and falling further and further away.

At dinner earlier, his client kept asking the waitress if the falls were like disney world – were they recycling the water with a pump? When do they close the falls for maintenance? And Mark kept laughing too hard, trying to flatter his client, embarrassed with himself for being such a phony. During dinner, he kept looking out the window at the lit-up ferris wheel. He kept thinking of the native americans who had once lived here, within the roar and mist of these falls. He wondered what the indians would think of the fireworks, the casinos, the rotating colored lights. Of men who made their livings with fake laughter.

Something was wrong. All this man-made flair was here to celebrate a miracle of nature, and yet nothing seemed natural. The falls should have been left alone, pristine and unscarred by hotels, casinos, and fireworks. Niagara falls was a symptom of a disease that men carried inside them and passed down to every generation. It was an illness of the mind that made men believe everything had to be improved, but everything they touched only became worse, a perverted facsimile of the original. *Like my soul, everything here has gone off course, tilted away from what is real, from the innocence that was there, to something distorted that worships all the wrong things.*

He kept thinking of that tiny girl from the sandwich place last week. Her eyes were crossed. She was so ugly he had to look away from her. *What was it like to live your whole life with everyone avoiding eye contact with you?* he wondered. She never looked directly at him, and Mark realized she probably knew that she was ugly and deformed – people must have told her that at some point. And yet she was still nice to him and asked him politely what he wanted on his sandwich.

The girl had kept ruining the white cheese slices, fumbling as she tried to separate them from each other. He'd looked away, hoping to give her a better chance of getting them separated. She was cursed by her crossed eyes and poor coordination. She looked seventeen or eighteen, supposedly going into the prime of her life; but her life would only get worse; she would only get uglier and more uncoordinated as she aged.

The falls and the girl depressed him. Both were cursed by modern life. There was no hope in this glittering new world for anyone with crossed eyes and fumbling fingers. Beauty, ability, and profit were all that mattered. She probably believed that someday someone would finally love her instead of just feeling sorry for her, but that was impossible in this age. Her life would always rely on the kindness of others, never their honest respect and admiration.

Room service came, and a so-so girl delivered a silver bucket filled with ice and six coors lights with french words on the labels. Also on the tray were two pilsner glasses and a glass with ice and brown liquid, which he assumed was the crown royal he'd ordered. It all totaled sixty bucks, which was ridiculous, but he signed the bill and added a ten-dollar tip to it.

What would the indians think? Years ago, the men living by these falls didn't know about whiskey, or cans of beer, or fireworks, or colored electric lights; they knew only water and moonlight and the unceasing roar of the falls. Even though he was six floors up in the marriott, he felt the native american spirits all around him. This must have been holy ground to them, a place where they would sit and wonder and try to understand the incomprehensible world. But tonight, he and civilization and capitalism were defecating on their ghosts.

At the business dinner, at the urging of Paul, the canadian sales director, he had sneaked silverware and a salt shaker into the client's laptop bag. Apparently, it was some big inside joke: airport security would find the utensils and salt shaker, continuing a long-running gag.

Business was all a crazy, trivial game, like a child obsessively tying and retying his shoes over and over in a corner. They would diagnose the child with autism for that behavior, yet people obsessed even more single-mindedly about business – the stock market, the federal reserve, the unemployment rate, the economic implications of the upcoming election. It all seemed important, but hundreds of years from now, none of those things would matter. History was riddled with financial ups and downs, pathetic politicians, fortunes, and ruin. All that truly mattered was the truth, and everyone was so far from it that there was no hope. *Society is autistic*, Mark thought. *Collectively, we are focused on all the wrong things.*

What would the indians think? Their ghosts were here, all around him while he was going crazy wondering what his purpose was. Their purpose had been simple: to do real work, to love for real, to laugh for real. Mark's purpose was different – his survival was assumed, and so somehow his purpose included ferris wheels, casinos, cans of coors light, fake laughter, drinking crown royal, and watching colored lights rotate under the falls. It all summed up to nothing.

What would the indians think? He turned away from the hotel room window and looked at the nightstand beside the bed. The lampshade was a globe of red glass; it made him think of the war paint that indian braves put on their faces before going to battle.

He was barely holding on to both sanity and whatever was good inside him. Sixteen years ago, he'd decided to become a husband. Gaia was mostly happy. His four beautiful children were mostly happy. But his smile was painted on. Something wasn't right; inside he was white-knuckled, hanging off a ledge, trying not to let go, trying to pull himself up to be a good person. He wished he could go back and start again and hold on to love. But maybe he was too far gone. Maybe that was impossible.

What was Gaia doing right now, on the evening of their anniversary? The horrible thoughts taking over his mind made him miss her in a way that he hadn't for a long time. He was going off the rails inside. Something good was slipping away and being replaced with wickedness. If Gaia was here, he could cling to her and hold onto what virtue he had left before he lost it forever.

Tonight, there was no lust in him for once; he just wished that Gaia was here beside him on the bed. They could lie still, not speaking in the dark, holding hands and listening to the falls roar outside. And he knew that if she was here, she would squeeze his hand softly, and he would fall asleep believing he was sane and loved, instead of feeling crazy and so desperately alone.

FIVE
animalium

I can't believe I'm back in prison, Griffin Turner thought. *Please be a nightmare.* He pinched his fingertips together. It felt real. *I'm awake. This nightmare is real.* Here I am again, alone, trapped with animals. I'm an animal.

He realized now that inmates were animals: caged like beasts, fed like beasts, punished like beasts; sometimes the government slaughtered them like beasts – poisoned, electrocuted, gassed, hung, or shot. This realization shined a light on his past blindness. He'd been ignorant. But now he could see.

The belief that prison rehabilitated was complete fantasy, a lie told to slip past the fatal truth that the situation was hopeless. The idea of a better future after prison was a myth, perpetuated to keep control. Hope gave inmates some small motivation to be disciplined. If the truth were clearly known – that there was zero hope – riots would bring every prison crumbling down into blood-soaked rubble.

After he first got out of prison ten years ago, Griffin saw the truth: there was no future for any felon. An inmate could lift weights; he could become a jailhouse tattoo artist. He could fold laundry and stamp license plates. Where was the future in any of that? And even if a criminal was somehow miraculously rehabilitated, he could never find a normal job. In illinois, like other states, there was a lengthy list of jobs that were illegal for felons to hold; it included even the lowest-level occupations.

By law, illinois felons couldn't be movers, they couldn't be tattoo artists, they couldn't be roofers. A felon could never be a barber, a bus driver, a lab technician, a paramedic, a veterinary technician, a cab driver, an athletic trainer, a real estate broker, or a car salesman. It was illegal for a felon to be a *bingo number caller.*

It was all a bad joke, and the punchline was his life ripped apart. Yes, the crime was his fault, but the consequences so unreasonably outweighed the crime.

He'd gone nowhere in sixteen years, ending up right back in prison where he started. Just before he'd turned nineteen, he was busted with a big bundle of crack in a backpack. He was delivering for Balty, making money to take back to college after christmas break. He'd won a full tuition scholarship to the university of illinois; but he still needed money for his room, food, books, and partying. He hadn't even known what was in the backpack until the cop showed him.

So instead of moving back into his college dorm after christmas, he moved into menard correctional facility. His public defender convinced him to plead guilty in exchange for leniency, so there was no trial. He was convicted of felony drug distribution and sentenced to the minimum: twelve years in prison and a fifty thousand dollar fine – *some leniency*. He could never pay off the fine, but he'd served his prison time.

After six years, he'd gotten out on parole, but back on the streets, he realized he'd really gotten a life sentence. Worse than prison, worse than missing out on college, was the felony conviction. The felony showed up in every employment background check; no one would hire him. If somehow he ever did find a legitimate job, a big part of his salary would be garnished to pay his delinquent fine.

His college dreams disappeared. The university rescinded the scholarship, and a drug felon couldn't obtain government student aid or loans. Felons were permanent pariahs. He was completely fenced out of any opportunity to make a better life for himself, unless he worked outside the system.

The inmates around him talked. Listening in, Griffin remembered that the worst thing about prison was the ignorance that surrounded him, the insanity that permeated everything, everywhere. Everything turned over on itself. Madness became the reality. As time went on your own mind became ignorant and irrational as well, blending in with its surroundings.

Griffin listened in on the conversation between the two inmates standing closest to him, both black veteran convicts. They were rapping, trading stories to pass the time. That's all there was to do in this place – for years. The first man, Blue, had scars slashed in an X across his cheek and a chicago bulls tattoo on his forearm. The second man, Newsky, wore an eye patch over an empty socket, his visible eye was permanently bloodshot.

Blue said, "I heard stateville is like, one of the worst places you can go. They got the electric chair there."

"Stateville is real. It's for hardcore killas and rapists," Newsky said.

"It's nothin' to be played with," Blue said.

Newsky said, "Yeah, I ever tell you about my time there? Crazy. Even on my way, before stateville, when I go to court, people tellin' me how it's messed up. Then, when I leave court, at the county bullpen, there was this dude there. When it's time to go, he won' get cuffed up wit' nobody. Everybody gotta be cuffed up wit' somebody but he didn' wanna get cuffed up. The cee-oh was like, 'Dude c'mon, man. It's time to go!'"

"Yeah," Blue said.

"So everybody like, 'C'mon, man.' 'Cause he was wastin' time. So the cee-ohs start grabbin' him, and then he creased the cee-oh! I'm talkin' bout knocked the guard out on his *face*, bro! One of the cee-ohs, creased! Boom! So everybod–"

"How big was this dude that knocked the cee-oh on the ground?" Griffin interrupted.

Newsky turned and looked over at Griffin. "He was a *mexican*, bro! He wadn' that big – a li'l' scrawny dude. Knocked him – boom! I'm like whoa. I ain't never seen that before. So the guards beat him up good. We leave, and he's lyin' there bleedin', his head cracked open, not movin'. He ain't come with us. He stayed there dyin' and we left. So I'm like, the ride just gettin' *started* and one dude's already *dead*, you know what I'm sayin'?"

"Why'd you get sent there?" Griffin asked.

"Drugs. Same as every idiot. I was guilty under the law, but I'm innocent before god."

"How so?" Griffin asked, curious.

"Follow me, bro. If I carry crack in my pockets for my posse, I'm a criminal. If I'd started a company and cooked up ritalin for millions of little first graders, I'd be a big shot, hundred percent legit, a contributin' member of society. I'd donate to politicians; I'd be a patron of charities."

"Yeah, but you didn' start no company." Blue laughed. "You were on the street."

"Exactly! You can deal drugs to kids if you got a license from the government – then the crime's legal."

"Tell that to the judge." Blue laughed.

"Listen, break it down. Dealin' is commerce – buyin' and sellin' – just capitalism. That ain't wrong. Ok, so it's the drugs that makes it wrong. But drugs alone ain't a crime. In most cases, drugs are legal if a pharmacist deals 'em; so it ain't drug dealin' that's immoral, just the circumstances of it."

"Same story," Griffin said. "My crime was being stupid. I wish I'd known at eighteen just half of what I know now. I was blindsided. We spent all that time learnin' state capitals; they should have held a school assembly tellin' everybody to never talk to cops without an attorney. Look around here; seems like all the white people had that class."

Blue and Newsky laughed.

Griffin continued, "I got out of prison the first time and I couldn't get a decent job; without that, I couldn't get a decent place to live; without that, I couldn't get a decent woman. Strike one, strike two, strike three. I was out. My options were zero. So I opened the one door I could still walk through. I started seriously dealin', built an empire in my hood, then expanded beyond. I was rollin' in dough, but got busted again. Now I'm back here in menard. Just possession though. I kept my mouth shut and had the benjis for an awesome lawyer this time. So I should get out in a year, maybe less."

"I hope you do, bro," Newsky said.

"Stateville," Griffin prompted.

Newsky said, "So I get to stateville. The bullpen cage has holes in it, and these *birds* were flyin' aroun'. *Birds* flyin' around the bullpen! I'm like, what? Like birds! Not *one* bird, like *birds* was flyin'."

"Crazy, dude. Did they check y'all before you got in the bullpen?" Blue asked.

"They did. So we get to the bullpen, an' birds flyin' aroun' an' we just sit there for a bit. Then they get us up, they search us. They make us strip naked, and they like, 'Drop all your clothes' – know what I'm sayin'? 'Bend over, spread your cheeks and hold 'em open wide.' Then this lady cee-oh walkin' past, she's lookin' at us naked all up in there, shinin' her flashlight and pokin' her baton in there while we hold ourselves open, so I'm like, *what?*"

"Y'all get searched at one time?" Blue asked.

"Yeah," Newsky said. "Lined up, bent over, and held open, straight-up creepy. And the cee-ohs yellin', 'Open it up! Open it up!' After that we get in the shower, all of us get in the shower. We had to. I didn't wanna but you go through that phase where you just gotta – it's to the point where you *got* to. So, man, we get in the shower, and I'm jus' not even showerin'. I'm jus' tryin' to get through the process. Dudes *lookin'* at dudes, talkin', makin' jokes. I'm like, man, these dudes is clowned out. After that, we sleep in the bullpen for the whole weekend."

"And the birds was just flyin' in the air?" Blue asked.

"Birds was just flyin'! These birds poopin' constantly, birds poopin' all over." Newsky sniffed and wiped his nose with the back of his arm. "And in stateville we ate bad, know what I'm sayin'? I didn' like to eat the food. They was servin' us *hot dogs* every mornin'!"

Blue laughed, and Griffin smiled at Newsky's passionate disgust.

"We ate breakfast at four in the mornin', we ate lunch at ten, and we ate dinner at four. So it was like weird times. And, dude, they gave us hot dogs every mornin'. They givin' us hot dogs every mornin' and brothers was tweakin' out, goin', 'Man, we just ate this!'"

"Right, right," Griffin said.

Newsky was excited, his hands waved in front of him while he spoke. "Some dudes are throwin' hot dogs at the birds. They tweakin', bro! So then I start tweakin'. I'm like, this is crazy. I'm laughin', I'm thinkin' this is funny as hell. Then after the weekend, they got us outta the bullpen and I go to a cell. It's loud – everybody screamin', bangin' on their doors. Dudes throwin' books. G-crazy!"

"Savages, bro," Blue said.

"Like you said, it's everybody at once, it's killas, robbas, everybody at once, rapers. It's everybody in the same place at once."

Blue was laughing. "Straight savages, bro!"

Newsky continued, "So I started rotatin' with a brother. We used to get snacks. They still feedin' us hot dogs – but we used to get snacks. I started gamblin' my snacks. Usually, we'd gamble for these little cookies we used to get. But the day that I *lose,* we got *chips,* and we never got chips. So I'm like, we got chips, and I owe this brother my snack!"

"Word," Griffin said.

"So when they came with the chips, he slant in on me like I owed him a thousand dollars. So I'm like, 'Man, you know we don' ever get chips. I got you on two – I'll give you two snacks instead of this one chips.' 'Cause we ain't never had chips and I'm so hungry. So he like, 'Man you tryin' to play me like a hoe?' I'm like, 'Man, it ain't like that. I got you on *two other* snacks.' Then he snatched the chips outta my hand – know what I'm sayin'? Snatched the chips outta my hand! I'm like, what? He snatched the chips and I was on the bed when he did it. So I get up, and soon as I get up, he swings on me – *boom!* So me an' him fightin' an' I slam him on the groun'. Then some brother that he knew came up and started hittin' me from the back!"

"Oh no!" Blue exclaimed.

"They move on me, and I ain't get my chips back. I'm mad and I knew what I was gonna do. We was in the dorm, so when dudes sleep – whoever's asleep, you could just walk up to their bunk an' just do whatever, if it came down it. And that's what it came down to.

"So that night, I go up to the brother's bed an' I snatch his cover off his head and I start goin' on him – boom, boom, boom – start goin' in. I'm creasin' him up somethin' good! I creased him up quick. Beat 'im up! So after that, I was really ready to go. 'Cause I was gettin' hassled by two brothers, and I was hungry. Everybody was hungry. They wadn' feedin' us right. It was just a messed up situation. Real messed up. And the cee-ohs finally called my bag. After me and him fought again, they called my bag."

"So now it's time to get outta there," Blue said.

"Yeah, now it's time to go. I'm like, ok, I'm cool. He *did* keep the chips, but I didn' go out like no girl. So my ride at stateville was over. I was so happy to go. Man, it was just real messed up. Not eatin', dudes comin' in the shower on you, everybody fightin', poppin' pills every day, like no sleep–"

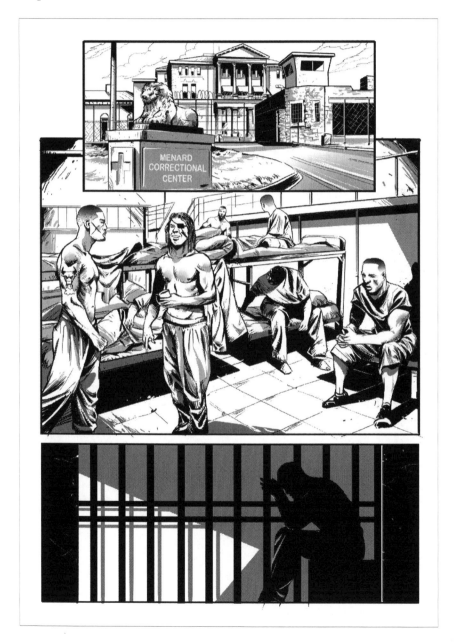

"How was they gettin' pills in there?" Griffin asked.

"Cause dudes really got issues. When they go to the joint, they get checked out, they see the psychiatrist, and they prescribe 'em with these *hardcore* drugs, dope that's harder than xanax and all that."

"That's wild," Griffin said.

"Yeah. Stateville is bad. I never want to go through that again – ever, never *ever*. Like, for anybody. I wouldn't want anybody else to go through that. It was real messed up. I'd rather die than go back. That place is the real deal. I'm tellin' you."

Blue said, "Sounds like every prison. Rule number one is the strong prey on the weak. Rule number two is abandon hope. When in doubt of the other rules, see rules one and two."

This is hell, Griffin thought. His heart suddenly ached with disgust at the nonsense that permeated everywhere. He put his head in his hands. *This is hell.* Spending eternity listening to stories about drugs, birds, hot dogs, and never-ending wars of violent revenge over a bag of potato chips. He wanted to cry with desperation. He was thankful that it was impossible for him to cry; all his tears had been used up. He could never show the weakness of tears in front of these vicious inmates.

When he got out of prison again, he had to do something different. He had to get away from all this and do something where he was his own man, in charge of his own life. He had to do something where he could be free for the first time. He had no clue how to get it, but simple freedom was his persistent prayer – freedom from his past mistakes, freedom to make a decent living.

Freedom to be a man.

SIX
no law

Everything Hitler did in Germany was legal.
          – Martin Luther King

Excerpt from the textbook, *Origin, Evolution, and Current Principles of the American No Law Movement, Fourth Edition,* by Sean McClusky.

Introduction
The disintegration of the United States of America into today's loosely bound confederation of independent nation-states was the result of the No Law movement that began in the twenty-first century. Within thirty-five years of the first No Law rally, the United States transformed from a strong centralized authority ruling over fifty states into today's loosely knit confederation of fifty-six independent nations who voluntarily associate with each other to facilitate cross-border trade, environmental regulation, and the extradition of fugitives.

No Law leadership believed in an America without federal law. They believed the highest authority should be state government, with the states then delegating their authority to counties and towns, creating thousands of unique experiments in governance across the country. The No Law platform rebelled against a national "one size fits all" government. No Law leaders fought for local innovation. They argued for local iterations of failure and success, with failed experiments abandoned and successes adopted and refined.

No Law leadership argued that the internet made large government unnecessary. The ability for individuals to collaborate instantaneously obliterated the antiquated need for coordination by a federal government system that was developed before the telegraph. No central authority or meeting place was needed to unite individuals across geographies. Post-internet, people could communicate and negotiate directly online, without elected representatives travelling thousands of miles and without laws distorted by the influence of corporate lobbyists who roamed the halls of government.

The two sacred No Law values are "liberty and truth", captured in the movement's Latin motto, "*libertas et veritas*". The No Law leader Declan Kikas explained in an interview, "Everything starts with liberty, with freedom. Everything. Freedom to say what you want to say, freedom to do what you want to do. Our two highest values are liberty and truth. Liberty is first – because truth follows freedom."

Outline
This text will explore how and why the No Law movement brought down the most powerful nation in history, not through force, but through a peaceful, populist uprising that has inspired other local government movements throughout the world. Subsequent chapters will examine:

Mass incarceration: The United States had become the world's largest jailer, with increasing imprisonment of nonviolent drug offenders by for-profit corporations.

Meddling foreign policy: The United States had the world's largest military and interfered across the globe. At its peak, America had over eight hundred foreign bases with U.S. soldiers stationed in over one hundred and fifty foreign countries. The United States had more bases in foreign lands than any other empire in history, costing taxpayers trillions of dollars. America's foreign meddling resulted in constant retaliatory attacks by terrorists.

Corporatism: The No Law movement constantly attacked the notion of legally sanctioned corporations for multiple reasons. Corporations allowed people to profit from their actions without being held responsible for them. Corporations influenced federal law through large political donations and were given federal assistance not available to individuals. No Law leaders argued that corporations were pathological entities that manipulated public policy, plundered natural resources, and exploited workers without any moral restraint.

Declining states' rights: The federal government overrode state laws and sovereignty across a range of issues as trivial as the drinking age to larger issues such as education and healthcare.

Religious and ideological sects: Fundamentalist religious groups and ideological sects took control of local governments across the country. These groups included militant Amish in the Great Lakes region around Ohio, Mormons in the Rocky Mountain states around Utah, Hasidic Zionists in northeast urban areas, fundamentalist Christians in the plains states and rural southeast, libertarian "free staters" in New Hampshire, and pockets of fundamentalist Islamists throughout the country. Inner-city gangs, "Black Lives Matter" activists, and outlaw motorcycle gangs grew in membership, territory, and power. As local politics became more segmented by sectarianism, there was increasing pushback against the federal government.

Media consolidation: In the twenty-first century, a small number of large corporations controlled news and entertainment. The No Law movement provided alternative reporting and opinion through their LeV (Libertas et Veritas) network. The LeV network circumvented federal microaggression laws by making every broadcast a parody, which the U.S. Supreme Court ruled was protected by the First Amendment. LeV produced a continuous stream of content that satirized federal authority and convinced many people to join the No Law movement.

Daylight savings time: No Law leadership used the six-year political battle over daylight savings time to their advantage – pointing out the absurdity of the federal government being log-jammed by its own bizarre creation.

Monetary policy: The federal government, via the Federal Reserve bank, created trillions of dollars out of thin air to bail out large corporations. Large companies borrowed at ultra-low interest rates while individual citizens had to pay much higher interest. Citizens constantly lost money due to inflation and were burdened by large, long-term loans to purchase a house, a car, or an education. Many Americans struggled with staggering education loans their entire lives since under federal law school loans could never be discharged in bankruptcy.

National debt: The national debt had grown to over twenty trillion dollars in the early twenty-first century, a debt of over sixty thousand dollars per American. No Law leadership proclaimed that no individual had an obligation to pay the debts of past generations, especially since federal government spending was controlled by corporate lobbyists.

Domestic terrorist attacks: Terrorist attacks inside the country increased in frequency and severity. The Oklahoma City bombings, the World Trade Center and Pentagon attacks of two thousand one, and the coordinated nuclear attacks in New York, Los Angeles, and the District of Columbia – all supported the No Law argument that the federal government was not only incapable of keeping America safe, but its meddling foreign policy and unfair treatment of citizens was the very reason that America was constantly under attack.

Foundations

Declan Kikas is regarded as the founder of the No Law movement. He argued that government has an inherently evil influence on society and that it perpetuates abuses of power, dependency, and ignorance. Kikas denounced federal law, corporations, and central banking. He believed that federal authority limited the ability of individuals to use trial and error to improve local government. He argued that big government limited free exercise of private judgment. He believed that wisdom came from individuals acting freely, saying, "Liberty is the father of truth."

Kikas, an accomplished engineer and computer scientist, believed that the use of logic by the masses would eventually cause all big governments to wither away. Although he thought that the federal government was illegitimate, he was against using force to remove it from power. Rather, he advocated for revolution through a peaceful process, beginning with states holding democratic referendums to invalidate federal laws, leading opponents to coin the label "No Law" in an effort to disparage the movement.

Kikas argued that liberty was the only bulwark against the corruption of power. His opposition to the federal government and corporations inspired the No Law movement and made him one of the most influential philosophers in all of human history.

Fourth Edition

This text, now in its fourth edition, has become regarded as the definitive academic exploration of the No Law movement. Subsequent chapters will introduce the reader to more extensive review and discussion of No Law methods and theory. It documents and analyzes the No Law philosophy, beginning with its early origins, and examines the future of a movement that is now spreading rapidly across the world.

SEVEN
first session

The psychiatrist interrupted, "So after hearing all this, I have to ask, why isn't Mark here?"

Gaia Halberstam leaned back into the large leather arm chair, crossed her coltish, fit legs, and answered, "He's out of town. He travels all the time for business. And he'd never talk to a stranger about his problems. He has a hard enough time talking with *me*. He doesn't even know I'm here. He'd be upset if he knew. He doesn't think there's anything really wrong between us."

"So maybe there isn't?" The psychiatrist looked young, twentyish, except for his full gray beard, and several age spots on his hands, which together indicated he was probably twice as old.

"Him not thinking anything's wrong is a sign that things are *horribly* wrong. If we see things that differently, can we really know each other? And if we don't know each other, can we be in love?"

"Don't be too hard on yourself, or him. No one truly knows themselves, so it's impossible to truly know another person. Love isn't knowing; it's believing and holding on. Let me ask, how is your love life?"

She looked towards the large window, studying the upper east side walkups across the street. "Up and down. Sometimes incredible, sometimes nonexistent. But even when we're together, more and more it's like we're not even together. Like he's with me, but I don't have his attention."

"What do you mean?"

"I think he's become like most successful men. I think he never truly connects with people in a genuine way because to be successful, you have to take from others more than you give. You have to be wary. You have to leave others behind. You have to be willing to let them struggle and suffer while you move ahead. Maybe it's impossible to be really successful and be truly empathetic. And I didn't realize that when we met. I didn't really think about it until after years of being with Mark. He does care somewhat, but mostly it's a show of caring, which makes him sociopathic, right?"

"I can't say that without knowing him more. I can say that we all have to be somewhat selfish to survive. It's just a matter of degree."

Her hands rubbed together lightly, one working its way around her wedding band, as if checking it was completely there. "There are just so many things I used to be absolutely certain of, that now I realize I was always wrong about. I keep wondering, what else am I wrong about?"

"When you try to talk to Mark about this, what does he say?"

"He's so moody and withdrawn that just having a real conversation with him requires perfect timing. I mean, lately, he's been absolutely stoic, hardly talking to anyone. A few days ago, I asked him why he hasn't been talking to me. He was annoyed by the question, but in the course of the conversation, he said, 'Most of what I say is lies, which I feel bad about. So the less I speak, the less I feel bad.' I mean, *wow.*"

"It sounds like he's under incredible stress."

"Yes. That's true. He's always working. *Always.* He has so many problems to deal with – employees, customers, the government – his entire existence is a negotiation, and most people couldn't live like that for a week. Years of it have changed him so much from the boy I met in college. I mean, he's a completely different person."

"And you?"

Gaia was quiet for moment. Her fingers drew crooked circles on the armrests. Then she leaned forward and looked directly at the man. "I've changed, but I'm not different. Does that make any sense? I mean, if you met me twenty years ago and you met me now, within an hour you'd know I was the same person. If you met the two Marks, you'd never be able to guess that today's Mark is even the same species as the boy I first kissed in the back of a station wagon."

"Yes, I understand what you're saying. Well, Gaia, there's a lot we can dive into here. I do think it would help you to talk more about all this. To take things apart, sort through them, and piece them back together with some outside perspective, and with tools that I can give you. So if you want to meet again, or start meeting regularly, we can set that up."

"Yes. I want to do that. I need to." She smiled hopefully.

"Ok, good. Thanks, Gaia."

"Thank you, doctor. I really appreciate it."

EIGHT
eidolon

Mark Halberstam lay still, mostly asleep, partially wrapped up in a white, soft blanket. A woman was sleeping beside him. *Her name? Her name? Her name?* Sheila, that's right, Sheila. *How do I keep forgetting that?* His mouth tasted horrible and he remembered vodka tonics and cigarettes. Ugh. Alcohol, quinine, and nicotine. Dirt tasted better. Idiot. Every brilliant idea from last night seemed stupid this morning.

The supermodel Sheila was fast asleep, her back towards him. Her shoulders and neck were perfectly formed and her tousled, brown-black hair glowed in the first morning light. He felt himself becoming aroused just watching her sleep.

The dawn's brilliance stopped behind the fabric blinds, casting a yellow glow across the room. He closed his eyes, then barely opened them. His sleepiness was like breathing a gas that calmed him. He looked up, and saw a chipmunk perched on a shelf a few feet away. It turned and the creature's impish black eyes looked into his.

Why is there wildlife inside a luxury new york city hotel? I should call the front desk.

The animal had brown fur with black stripes running from its neck to its tail, which curled around off the side of the shelf. The chipmunk looked like an old soul with unearthly knowledge to share. He hadn't seen a chipmunk for years. He remembered seeing one on a hike with the kids once. The chipmunk tilted its head and looked off, staring intently towards the side of the room.

Mark looked that direction and saw an older man standing close to the bed. He stood erect, wearing a suit coat over a collared shirt with no tie, and his full gray hair and intense stare made him look almost demonic, like an evil apparition that had travelled through dimensions and outside of time to

42

speak to him, to tempt him and convince him to finally give up any pretense of self-control. Or was the old man an angel? Sent there to save him. *Or maybe I'm just dreaming,* Mark thought. *Maybe there is no chipmunk, maybe there is no man standing here in front of me.*

The old man stepped towards the bed and said, "Listen Mark, nothing from the past can control you, once you realize that you're free. Everything is brand new. Nothing that you've done, or that anyone else has ever done, can have power over you."

Mark pushed himself up, sitting shirtless, his arms flexed in case the man tried to do something. He looked over at Sheila. She was still asleep. Then he looked back at the man. "But aren't we all connected – to each other and to our past?" Mark asked.

"Yes, but both can only push us forward. They can never slow us down or hold us back unless we let them, don't you understand that?"

"What about my parents? They have expectations of me."

"You have no parents anymore. Your parents are someone else's parents because you are a different person than the one they gave birth to. You give birth to your new self each moment."

The old man continued, "The biggest curse is guilt. The second biggest is expectation. And you perpetuate it all upon yourself. You must break free. You should know that you are already free from any guilt or expectation."

"No. I'm not. Gaia and our kids, they rely on me. They rely on me to set an example for them. They rely on me to put a roof over their heads, pay for food, clothing, shelter, education, healthcare; their entire existence relies on me. And beyond that, they rely on me to learn about the world – responsibility, love, commitment, hard work."

"You've given them that. You're done, Mark. Leave Gaia. Leave your children. They're young adults now, capable of learning for themselves and taking care of themselves. You aren't helping them; you're imprisoning them. You need to free them to be themselves, or else they will imagine they have an obligation to you. Your charade gives them false expectations to live up to, and they will be tied to the past by the same imaginary ropes of guilt that bind you. These fake ropes appear real and strong because they are woven across time, but they can be cast off in an instant. Everything you think you're tied to is in the past but read the bible. Christ says we must be born again to be saved. A newborn baby has no guilt. He is innocent of any sin, free of any responsibility to others. You are newly born every moment, if you choose to be."

"I'm not sure I believe in Jesus."

"Then believe in me, and what I'm telling you. The most loving parents commit murder with smiles on their faces. They force us to destroy the person we really are: a subtle kind of murder."

"I think I've heard that before," Mark said.

"James Morrison said it," the old man replied. "And you remember it because you've always known it's true."

"James Morrison? Isn't he with goldman sachs? Or wait, morgan stanley?"

"The doors a prophet walks through aren't important. What's important is his message. Lying is the only sin there is. Everything else is an honest mistake to be learned from. Never turn a mistake into a sin by lying about it."

Mark said, "Well, sometimes lies keep other people from being hurt. Gaia would be heartsick if she knew that I was in bed with another woman. She thinks I'm out of town on business. This whole thing is crazy. I'm a jerk."

"Gaia has been hurt already by your mistakes. She just incorrectly believes she hasn't."

"Well, I can't leave her. I do love her. No. I need to stop messing around with Sheila and recommit myself to Gaia and start over. I can be born again that way, by learning from my sins – or my mistakes, as you call them – and not making them again."

The old man didn't answer.

Mark looked away from the man, over at the bookshelf, and the chipmunk was gone. He looked at Sheila; she was still asleep. He looked back at the man and now there was no one there. He lay back down, confused and tired, staring intently at the hotel room ceiling. The sound of Sheila's soft, gentle breathing calmed him and led him back into sleep.

When he woke up later the old man was still gone, but the memory of the dream stayed with him.

NINE
sunset strip

I get this feeling like
it all could happen
that's why I'm leaving

— Lana Del Ray, *West Coast*

Griffin Turner looked around. *This bar is a dump*, he thought. The red semi-shag carpet had a permanent layer of crust on it. Everything smelled stale. Even the freshly brewed coffee tasted old. It was pointless to come here every afternoon.

He hadn't realized how gross this place was until he came here sober. He'd quit drinking three days ago, and now what had been boozily blurry came into focus. He'd been mistaken: the red carpet wasn't luxurious; it was a crusty, stained disaster. The women here weren't looking for his companionship, but his money. They weren't laid-back; they were exhausted. And their looks didn't hold up well under a sober gaze. Without beer goggles, the view was disheartening.

But Griffin didn't leave. He had nothing to do and tons of cash to burn, and this place was good for wasting money and time. He'd come to los angeles to find freedom and a fresh start. He'd found this west hollywood bar instead.

He looked at his phone, then his coffee, then his phone. He wanted a cigarette, but he was too lazy to go outside and hide in between buildings from the overreacting west hollywood health nuts who threw tantrums whenever their aligned chakras were mangled with secondhand smoke. He coughed and felt stuff loosen in his lungs and clump up into the back of his throat. He pulled an already moist tissue from his pocket, spit up some sludge, and examined it. The snot was thicker than yesterday, and looking greenish now, which couldn't be good. The goopy pudding coming out his lungs was another excuse to hold off on having a cigarette.

The music blared too loud while a white girl with stringy brown hair, glazed-over eyes, and an amazing body gyrated in front of him. He put a pile of one-dollar bills on the edge of the stage as Karen Overton's voice sang from the speakers and the lyrics danced through his thoughts...

> *Sometimes the way that you act makes me wonder,*
> *what I am to you.*
> *Sometimes I can't stand the way that I'm acting,*
> *to be part of the things you do...*

Hollywood was home this fall. He'd gotten out of prison last spring and came to california after spending the summer in upstate new york, an hour south of the canadian border – a border with more holes than a donut factory. He'd spent the summer going up to montreal every few weeks, loading up on drugs at way below wholesale. The french and italian smugglers in montreal had so much stuff, and were so scared of the canadian mounties, that they sold on slim margins to anyone buying in bulk.

They had gobs of heroin and coke, but also tons of synthetics – new chemicals he'd never even heard of – which were big moneymakers. The newer a drug was, the more demand there was for it, and the more he could charge – a lot more. Everyone wanted a new high. Everyone wanted to feel different than they'd ever felt before.

He'd spent most of his summer stockpiling, but he dealt also, sitting in a run-down dive bar, selling baggies of dope to locals. When the weather was good, he sat at a table that was open to the outside, right up against the sidewalk. The dive bar was his office. He sat there all day, sipping ice-cold three-dollar pints of miller light and listening to the grateful dead that the bartender kept on permanent rotation; the dead's jams mixed with the constant clack of pool balls and the grunted conversations of the loafing drunks.

Griffin did enough retail business to pay for his furnished apartment and his day-to-day expenses, while investing his profits into loading up a u-haul truck with high-quality pharmaceutical contraband, preparing for a big west coast run. He'd planned on a six-figure payoff at the end of the summer after he took the stockpiled drugs on a cross-country selling tour.

In front of him, the glazed-eyed, dancing brunette rotated her bottom up, down, and around… up, down, and around... up, down and around... and it hypnotized him. He pushed some dollar bills towards her.

The brunette reminded him of his dream last night. In his dream, he'd been walking around a merry-go-round and saw a young woman with orange pigtails sitting on a ceramic horse. She wore pink lipstick and reflective sunglasses.

"I don't know what I'm doing here," Griffin had said to her.

"No one asked," she answered him. "And no one else does either. It's all a bunch of up, down, and around, you know." She waved her arms, gesturing. Griffin had looked around and saw that the merry-go-round was floating, hovering somehow in the sky with nothing underneath it, with nothing in sight but a few wispy clouds and blue atmosphere.

"Do you hear piano chords?" he asked her.

She looked at him and said, "Yeah, and I hear a saxophone also. It's like a pattern that's trying to communicate some kind of a message. I mean, there's some kind of love in all of us. I know there is love in each of us. And you never know what love can do. I've got a soul and you've got a soul and something gave us our souls."

"I'm going crazy on this thing. I mean, what's next? Just ride around in fear of falling off? I've seen everything. Nothing new is going to happen."

"Ok."

"So I'm stepping off," he said.

"It doesn't matter," she replied. "If we've lived a moment, then we've lived forever."

"Bye," he said. He stepped towards the edge and grabbed a brass post, looking out over the side. The calm, clear blue was hypnotizing. He leaned over as far as he could, holding on tightly to the post while trying to look underneath, but he couldn't lean forward far enough to see what was under the carousel.

So finally he let go, not knowing for sure he was going to until he was already falling, floating away. He looked back and saw the girl with orange pigtails looking over the side, watching him fall, waving to him. Very soon the carousel became a dot, then it disappeared and he was alone, falling through the blue, blue, blue; he was twisting and turning and enjoying the feeling of stretching and bending weightlessly.

There was nothing around him, just eternal blue forever. Would he ever land? Would he ever see anything else? The blue blinded him after a while, and he wasn't sure if his eyes were open or closed, but he thought he heard a voice chanting, "*you, you, you, you, you, you...*"

He'd woken up from the dream soaked in sweat. He'd been sweating through his t-shirt every night – a consequence of too much alcohol along with the increasingly weird dreams that chased him. As soon as his eyes closed, he was trapped. His body rested while his mind was tortured.

His dreams were getting more disturbing and kept bringing uneasiness into his day because he spent the daytime taking apart the nighttime dreams. He would drink and disassemble them and look for clues, but he could never put all the pieces together in a way that made sense. His dreams made him feel detached, like a different species from those around him, like an independent observer, like an alien reporter sent to earth to contemplate, but never authentically participate.

It all summed up to really needing a drink. He'd been dry for three days now, and it became suddenly clear that temporary sobriety wasn't working. Resolved to start drinking again, Griffin got up from his seat near the dancing brunette and went to sit at the bar. He ordered a glass of jameson's irish whiskey and a bottle of labatt's canadian beer. *God save the queen*, he thought, looking at both drinks sitting in front of him.

Leaning against the bar, he looked over at a dancer named Cindy who was sitting beside him. She seemed drunk out of her mind, but she recognized him and started talking to him.

"My sister left me, Griff. She went to kentucky with some guy four days ago, leaving me alone to take care of the house," she complained. "I hate dancing except for when I get to talk with guys like you. I need dancing to pay all my bills. Life's expensive, you know?"

Griffin smiled at the friendly hustle. "I know," he said, then took a big drink of whiskey and a bigger drink of beer. Her face was so close to his while she confided in him and he was becoming aroused.

"I used to work at a trucking company for over two years before I realized I wanted a new job, so I started dancing."

Looking at her up close, Griffin realized she was older than he thought at first – early thirties, not early twenties.

Cindy introduced the guy next to her, who was also drunk, as her boyfriend of eight years. *Eight years,* she emphasized, and it became clear to him that there was a message of frustration in those two simple words – *eight years. Eight years* was a statement of despair and resentment and a question of *why can't this man get his act together and marry me?* Griffin wondered: Why hadn't this guy married her yet and saved her from the soupy nowhere land of being single for too long? And why would he let her dance? Or did he make her?

He could see into a crystal ball where Cindy was headed, where she would be if she didn't – *right now, this very night* – break up with her boyfriend, quit drinking, and leave this strip club, leave los angeles and drive, drive, *drive.* Drive somewhere different and new where she could be who she was again, instead of who she'd become. If she didn't leave *right now* he knew she would never stop drinking or dancing until it was too late. She would never leave her freeloading, drunken boyfriend, he would never marry her, she would never stop being angry at her sister, and she would keep doing this more and more – getting stumbling drunk, crying into the neck of a man who paid attention to her while her boyfriend glared at both of them, telling her, "Let's go Cindy, it's time to go. I'm leaving now whether you come or not. Hey Griffin, bring her home, would you?"

The boyfriend's words sent a wave of panic through Griffin. He could already see what would happen if he took her home: They would start kissing in the red glare of his pontiac's dashboard lights, and he would get under her shirt and maybe inside her pants just before she vomited white russians and popcorn all over the inside of his car and all over him. He could already smell it a tiny bit – a premonition of the vomited milk, kahlúa, and vodka stench that would soak into his clothes, his car, and his memories. He would drop her off at home covered in smeared puke, and her boyfriend of eight years would add her drunken sluttiness to the tally of sins he could never forgive, and the ice between them would become even more rigid and firm, thicker and more impenetrable while it locked them even tighter together.

"You need to *leave,*" Griffin said, and Cindy just looked at him. Her eyes looked deep into his and made him uncomfortable. "With your boyfriend," he added.

"Yeah, ok. See ya," Cindy said, grinning at him with a drunk, unfocused smile. She got up and left.

Now what? Griffin thought. A gorgeous, hispanic-looking dancer sat farther down the bar, texting. She must be broken, he thought. I just don't know how because I don't know her; I can only see her gorgeous outside. And the bartender with amazing breasts – she also has to be broken to work here, no matter how amazing her breasts are. And I must be broken to be sitting here. What am I looking for? Drunkenness? Excitement? Sex? Distraction? Each possibility pointed to him being an incomplete human being.

Whoever owns this place must also be broken, Griffin thought. What kind of person owns a strip club, a place that arbitraged the lust of men and the greed of women, profiting from both insatiable desires? The owner must be a man, Griffin thought. It's impossible that a woman could own a strip club. And this town, hollywood, must be broken to allow this place, and thus california must be broken, and so america is broken. And thus, god himself is broken to build a world where a strip club exists in even one place for one evening. *God is broken.* And if god is broken, if god himself is a sinner, then I can't be too hard on myself. *I'm in good company,* Griffin thought.

He suddenly felt drowsy, so he gulped down the rest of the whiskey and finished the beer to try and wake up. It didn't help. *People think too short-term,* he thought. Nothing is really ever ok because in the long run, we're all dead. Or maybe that's why that everything is ok. Or maybe we're all insane, so just live for today, keep it coming.

His thoughts were careening and he realized he'd drunk enough. He really had to stop drinking forever at some point.

He went outside and smoked a couple of cigarettes in a dark corner of the parking lot, inhaling, trying to hold the smoke in his lungs until maybe the webbing in his mind shifted and he could see things differently.

He needed to start over, he decided. Live a decent life. Get a good woman. Make an honest living. Stay out of prison. Stop drinking and drugging. Maybe even stop smoking. And for sure he had to stop dealing. He was playing with fire. California's *three strikes* law would put him in prison for at least twenty-five years if he got caught dealing here.

I don't know what to do, All I'm sure of is that I have no idea what to do. Everything appears to be optional. What is clarity? What is truth? Is it truly up to me to decide?

Griffin put out his cigarette and walked to his car. He knew one thing. It was time to go home.

TEN
secret truth

Ethan Halberstam lay on the couch, rubbing Mister Whiskers' belly. The dog nudged him when he stopped petting him for too long. He was supposed to be doing homework; it was only october, just two months into the school year and he was already so far behind in every class. But he couldn't focus on schoolwork. It was impossible to concentrate.

All he kept thinking about was mom and dad and wondering what it would be like if (*when?*) they divorced. In some ways, things would be the same. He rarely saw dad anyways. Dad was always travelling *(now you know why)*, and when he was home, he seemed completely checked out, thinking about work *(or his girlfriend!)*.

Day to day, life would be better with just mom. Dad was always stressed out, and his unease was contagious, infecting everyone around him with tension. He'd have more freedom without dad around. Mom was too trusting, whereas dad constantly cross-examined him.

But he loved his dad. He remembered one time dad took him to baseball practice and sat in a folding chair. Whenever he looked over, dad was watching and smiling. And dad loved his music, always encouraging him to write songs and play guitar.

But dad was cheating. He'd seen the texts on his phone. 'Unknown' was the header on the message list, but inside the message stream he'd learned that the woman's name was Sheila. Sheila texted pictures of herself. Sheila texted screenshots of flights she could take. Sheila wrote about the things that she would do to his dad when she got him alone.

And his dad texted back.

He'd found the messages a few weeks ago. Whiskers had grabbed a bag of deli ham off the kitchen table and dad set his phone down and ran upstairs after the dog. A text appeared on the screen. "It feels like a dream at times because the next day I wonder whether I was actually with you."

Without really thinking, he'd grabbed dad's phone and opened up his messages before the lock screen came on. Not believing his own eyes, and worried dad would come downstairs and catch him snooping, he'd quickly scrolled through recent texts, taking pictures of messages with his own phone. Now he sat there on the couch, weeks later, looking at some of them for the thousandth time.

His dad texted, "Hey beautiful Sheila, I keep thinking of you – weds could work for me, it's crazy soon, but crazy has worked well so far... something to think about :)"

Sheila answered, "I'd like to be wherever you are now."

His dad replied, "I wish that was true! It's only been a week but that seems too long ago!"

Sheila replied, "Just need to spend more than a day together. :) and this time put the 'do not disturb sign' on the door!"

His dad wrote, "yes! :)"

When Ethan heard dad coming downstairs, he quickly set the phone back, facedown. The discovery had stunned him, and he felt tears welling up. He didn't want dad to see him crying, so he walked into the dining room and leaned against the buffet, tears dripping down his cheeks.

While he cried, he remembered kicking the soccer ball with dad once when he was little. Ethan had looked up at him, talking and laughing with him, believing he was god, and knowing that the only thing that was important was to be perfect in his father's eyes.

Now he didn't know what to think of him. His father wasn't the man he thought he knew.

It was weird to think that only three people in the world – his dad, this woman Sheila, and him – knew this secret truth, a truth that would change everyone's life if it was ever revealed. His mom didn't know. His three sisters didn't know. This truth would change everyone's life in an instant.

But maybe it could remain a secret. Maybe his dad would stop messing around with Sheila and no one else would ever have to know. It could become like it had never happened.

Maybe he could find a way to get his dad to see he was being stupid. The sooner dad stopped cheating, the less chance there was of anyone else finding out. *Maybe, maybe, maybe – please god, please god, please god.*

Sheila was gorgeous. She looked like a model in her texted pictures. But his mom was the world's most beautiful woman *inside* – the kindest, most caring person ever.

It stressed him out. All he could think about was his dad cheating, his mom being betrayed, and his family disintegrating. He was in a daze at home and at school – missing assignments without knowing anything had been assigned. He was going to flunk every class, his already flimsy college resume would be permanently marred, and he'd end up at some mediocre community college. He was on a trajectory to join the teeming mass of unpersons, below average at everything, disappointing everyone.

It was bizarre, by keeping dad's betrayal secret, he was helping him continue to cheat. But he had to make sure that mom never found out. *Should I tell dad I know?* Ethan thought. *No, no, no. That would make this real. Our family would be damaged forever. Maybe instead, I can get him to see his mistake on his own (how?) or get him to fall back in love with mom (how?).*

Whiskers nudged him, and he scratched the dog's belly. If only the stupid dog hadn't stolen the deli ham, he thought. If only I wasn't a snoop. I could still be ignorant, and my life would be better. He wished he'd never picked up his dad's phone.

Ignorance is bliss, he thought. *But now I know the horrible truth, and I have to keep anyone else from ever discovering it.*

ELEVEN
goodbye

Mark Halberstam sat with his family at the dinner table. Gaia's crockpot stringed beef was delicious and his four children were smiling and laughing. It was a perfect may evening, and yet he couldn't enjoy it. *Think something nice... think something nice.* He couldn't stop his horrible thoughts. He was surrounded by love, yet cynicism and anger kept grasping at him.

Nothing was good enough, as if he was fixated on finding a few pieces of copper within a trove of gold. His mind skeptically examined everything good until it found the smallest imperfection, and then declared everything worthless as a result. His greed was also part of the problem. A pile of gold wasn't enough, he wanted a mountain; if he had a mountain, he wanted the world. His discontent kept getting worse. He had the best seat in the theater but kept looking for a better place to sit.

He was leaving town tomorrow and he had to admit to himself that he couldn't wait to go. He'd barely gotten home, but already needed to get away.

One of his biggest annoyances was how much Gaia spoiled the kids. They were never allowed to be upset, held responsible, or fail. Now, as young adults, they were confronting their inadequacies head-on, and the only tool in their skill box was turning to mom or dad for help. If he or Gaia couldn't fix it, the kids blamed them.

On friday afternoon, Gaia had forwarded him a text from their daughter, Julie. "Looks like I'm working this summer," it said, which meant Julie hadn't gotten accepted into the summer program at stanford. *Jesus.* Months of essays, applications, and standardized test preparation down the tubes. When he got home, Julie wouldn't talk to him; she was still pouting. Mark tried to hug her in the kitchen, but she rudely rushed past him.

Julie was one problem. A bigger problem was their only son, Ethan, who was handsome, talented, intelligent – but had become a chronic liar and pathologically lazy. Ethan was a sophomore in high school and at this point would be lucky to get hired at mcdonald's after graduation. He'd simply lost all motivation to do anything other than sit around in sweats, pet the dog, compose intricately picked songs on his guitar, nap, and play video games on his tablet.

Last semester, Ethan had gotten an f in biology; Mark was stunned by the failing grade. The rest of the report card was also dismal – d's and c's. He'd never seen an f on a grade card before. F's were given to life's ultimate losers – kids from alcoholic, broken families; kids with parents who didn't care. Failing took intentional, willful effort to not complete assignments and blatantly ignore work. When he investigated, he discovered that Ethan hadn't done any of the classwork. It was that simple.

Since the f, Mark put simple rules in place for the second half of the school year. Ethan wasn't allowed to leave the house or have any activities other than schoolwork, religion, tennis, and music lessons. Mark hired a private tutor who met with Ethan every afternoon.

Now it was may. Saturday morning, yesterday, he'd found out that Gaia had granted Ethan an exemption from months of grounding to go to his girlfriend's that night – without even checking with him. He was livid, but he'd let it go. He was going to let it slide until he asked Ethan if he was caught up on schoolwork. Ethan said he wasn't. *What?*

"How far behind are you?"

"I'm not sure. Pretty behind in everything," Ethan answered hesitantly.

He couldn't believe it. He found Gaia in the kitchen washing dishes. Good lord, couldn't she just let those sit until the maids were back on monday? She was always doing work that the overpaid housekeepers should be doing.

"There's no way Ethan's going to Sadie's. He's way behind on schoolwork."

Gaia looked into the sink when she answered, "He needs a break. He needs time with friends. He's been trapped here for months. We already told him he could go and–"

"*You* said he could go. *I'm* saying he'll stay home and work on schoolwork."

"No. It's ok for him to go," Gaia said.

Mark looked at her and her yellow rubber gloves moving amidst the soap suds. He hated her. All she did was undermine him. She was completely incapable of holding the kids accountable. Spoiled kids were cute when they were little, but now they were teenagers – almost adults – who had no chance of making it in the real world.

He returned to the family room to check on Ethan who was now wrapped up in a large, brown fleece blanket and had both his feet up on the desk. He was bobbing his torso forward, trying to get his hands over his feet so he could type on the keyboard.

"Get your feet off the desk!" Mark yelled. "If this is how you work, it's no wonder you can't get anything done. You can't even reach the keyboard. *Sit up* and work like a normal person!"

Ethan looked frightened, wary; he glanced at the fireplace, remembering, then he quickly sat up and put his feet on the floor.

"Show me the list of what you're behind on," Mark said.

Ethan's voice trembled, "I still need to make it."

Ethan wasn't going anywhere tonight, he'd decided. *No way.* He headed back to the kitchen to tell Gaia. "Ethan's *not* going out. The last quarter just started, and he's already behind. And he's been lying. I've asked him every weekend if he's caught up and he told me yes, but he's been behind the whole time."

"Do you know why he lies to you? It's because–"

Mark cut her off, "It doesn't *matter* what reason he has for lying."

"He's really struggling. He's been working as hard as he can for months, but he's not able to stay on top of it. He's working with the tutor and–"

"I don't care about all that," he said. "I'm–"

"Quit interrupting me! You're *always* interrupting me and I *hate* it and I can't take it anymore!" Gaia shrieked. He knew her tears would come soon.

"Ok, fine. Say what you want to say. I won't talk until you're done."

"I'm trying to tell you that he's scared to say he's behind because he knows how upset you'll be with him and it's *too much*. You get so upset with him."

Mark stormed out of the kitchen. It was impossible to reason with Gaia. He had to leave the room before the situation escalated into violence. Gaia was putting this on *him* – saying *he* was the reason that Ethan lied and was lazy. Gaia was nuts. Ethan was crazy. He had zero confidence in anyone's judgment; everyone's reasoning was suspect.

An hour later, Gaia came and found him. He'd been lying on the couch in his office, staring at the ceiling, an unopened book on his lap. Gaia kneeled beside the couch and said, "I do love you."

He felt some of his tension release, hearing her words, he softened for a moment – *maybe I'm too worked up?* – and smiled. "I love you too."

"This fight isn't what it seems. We both know this is between you and me."

"I don't know what you're talking about. It's about Ethan."

"Ethan told me he thinks we need to go to marriage counseling."

Of the seven million things Gaia could have said to him, she'd somehow found the worst. Violent anger rose up in him. He wanted to destroy and kill before retiring to a mountain cabin to drink whiskey alone; he'd guzzle his life away for three weeks before he died peacefully in his sleep from his liver exploding.

He sat up and hugged Gaia, forcing himself to be silent. This simple statement from their son was indicative of the whole problem. The brat had turned *his* lying laziness into an accusatory finger pointed at *their* marriage. Mark tried to speak calmly, "Gaia, this is *his* fault. If he wasn't lying, we wouldn't be fighting, and we wouldn't need counseling."

"That's not true."

"Gaia, I'm talking about him lying to me for *weeks*. For *months!*"

Gaia didn't say anything. She was infuriating, but Ethan was the problem, not Gaia. He needed to focus on Ethan. He'd gotten up and left Gaia to go confront Ethan again.

There was a good reason that Jesus was a bachelor and childless, he thought. Even god couldn't handle the unreasonableness of women and children. Marriage and fatherhood was a death march more torturous than any afternoon crucifixion. Jesus got off easy on the cross, he realized. Crucifixion was the wimpy way out. A family man suffered for life.

Mark had found Ethan still sitting at the desk in the family room, at least now giving the appearance that he was doing homework. "Listen, you're talking to your mom about *marriage counseling?*"

"Dad, I really need to tell you something. I–"

"No. *Shut up!* Listen to me. You've lied every time I asked you if you were caught up. You're telling your mom that *we* should go to *marriage counseling?* Is this about what I did to you a few weeks ago? I did that because I'm at the end of my rope with you, Ethan. I don't know what else to do. Listen, I'm sure our marriage could be better, but if you stopped *lying* and did *your schoolwork* we could skip a few counseling sessions because the reason we keep fighting would go away–"

"Dad, it's about– I keep thinking about something I sa–"

"All you keep thinking about is *yourself*, Ethan! Have you ever thought about what *you* can do to help *me?* It's simple – stop lying, do your homework. And *shut up*, talking to your mom about *marriage counseling*. I've got enough problems to deal with without your *stupid* input. How about this? Get a *c* in biology and then I might have some respect for your opinion. Until then, just *shut up* and do your homework!"

Ethan looked at the wall and quietly cried. *Good*, Mark had thought as he walked away. *Cry. It's time someone felt upset by all this other than me.*

That was last night. Now, sunday night, the tears had dried and everyone had calmed down. They were a loving family having a pleasant dinner together. He was doing his part by keeping his mouth shut. He just smiled, nodded, and made generically positive comments, forcing himself to ignore how his youngest, Beth, kept talking over everyone with food tucked into the side of her mouth like a gopher, a disgusting habit that Mark also had. It drove him nuts to see Beth doing the same thing.

Their second youngest child, Margaret, turned the dinner conversation to blacks. Blacks were still gunning each other down in chicago. The windy city bloodbath was worse than the middle east. And the blacks were still too poor. Everyone agreed with Margaret that something had to be done.

Mark simmered silently. Blacks annoyed him. They wanted something that could never happen: They wanted life to be fair, but everyone was a slave when they were poor and powerless. Everyone was discriminated against. *The blacks don't get it*, Mark thought. Rather than fight the righteous war for justice, the blacks needed to fight the selfish war for individual survival – each and every man for himself. The first war was unwinnable. The latter one could be won with hard work, luck, and greed. Protesting injustice was like protesting that two plus two equaled four – nothing would change it.

After dinner, sitting alone at the table, he decided to leave that night. He needed caribbean sunshine and a cold red-stripe beer – he could see the brown glass bottle with little beads of cold perspiration on it. Manhattan was unseasonably chilly and cloudy for the beginning of may, and the gray wasn't working. It was seeping into him, making him moody and resentful. Gaia and the kids were doing the best they could. They were all amazing and loving, and yet he sat through the meal upset with all of them because he was so unhappy with himself.

Their dog, Mister Whiskers, came up to him and leaned into Mark's leg. "Hey Whiskers, good boy." He petted the animal then got up and went to the kitchen and discovered Gaia and the kids planning a movie night with coffee and raspberry pie, but he said he had to pass. He went to his room instead and lay flat on the bed, staring at the ceiling and wondering if there was any way for things to be completely still. Not quite death, but not quite life either.

Could he just live alone in this bedroom? Like Howard Hughes trapping himself in the desert inn for years? He would communicate by sending notes under the door. His meals would be delivered by staff who never spoke to him, and all correspondence would be in writing. He would spend hours writing specifications for every detail of his food preparation: *"Take one del monte twelve-ounce can. First, take the paper label off the can of green beans. Wash the can in hot water at one hundred and seven degrees for three minutes..."*

He understood why Hughes had become a recluse. At some point it became necessary to maintain sanity. Many thought Hughes had lost his mind, that he ended up alone and neurotic in a dark hotel room because he'd gone crazy. But Mark realized that Hughes had done what was needed to *keep* his sanity. So many things were out of control, so many people wanted things from him, so many details could never be pinned down; Hughes needed *something* he could control, even it if was just a can of green beans.

Mark thought about the netherlands. Two weeks ago, he'd snuck away with Sheila and flown to the netherlands for a music festival called *'the state of trance'*. Sheila loved electronic music, so he took her to impress her. He remembered a performance by two hooded men on a platform. The men didn't sing, play instruments, or speak – they simply bobbed rhythmically in black robes, their faces hidden except for their mouths. Instead of guitar strings and piano keys, they touched dials and screens that manipulated the music, images, and laser lights. All the music was artificial, a collage of prerecorded soundtracks. The hooded artists on stage could have been imposters because no one could even see their faces. The real artists could have been in a different city, or even dead, and no one would know. It was possible that every part of the experience, except the crowd itself, was counterfeit.

At times, Mark had gotten into it. The screens around him filled up with blue and white sparkling lines. A woman's voice sang, *"All your dreams are dying... there's never enough, there's never enough..."*

He'd closed his eyes, then opened them, and stopped being able to tell the difference between when his eyes were open and closed as he lost himself in the music with everyone around him, lost together on a planet that made no sense at all, except for this one night when music led them to forget the never-answered questions that haunted all their souls. *"And we're gonna let it burrrrrn burn burn, we're gonna let it burrrrrn burn burn..."* And Mark had sung along with the woman's voice, joining her plea to let it all burn.

He remembered seeing an american flag glowing – actually lit up – on a man's t-shirt, and he saw that the american flag was still a beacon of freedom, still a middle finger to the rest of the world. *There's still hope for all of us,* Mark had thought, *and so there's still hope for me.*

Sheila had looked incredible in a pink sequined bikini top. He hadn't been able to take his eyes off her, and neither could other men. Part of him had been jealous when he saw men ogling her, and part of him hoped he might lose her to one of them. Another man would be a good way to end it because he wouldn't be able to get rid of Sheila easily. He should have learned by now that the more easygoing a woman seemed to be, the more she became a stage-five clinger at the end. The good-time party-girl facade always fell away to reveal a grasping, unstable mess. The more time they spent together, the more drama there would be when he replaced her. If Sheila found someone else, it would end easier. He could act hurt and she would run from him. Otherwise, it was going to be very messy.

Sheila didn't love him; even if she thought she did, she couldn't love him because she'd never known anything with him other than good times. She loved *being with* him, which was different. More precisely, she loved the accouterments that he provided: the private jet, the yacht, the first-class hotels. She'd been with him long enough that she thought of those things as hers. She'd be upset when he dumped her, mistaking her greed for his lifestyle with love for him. And she knew enough about him that she could cause serious damage. She'd be hard to control.

He opened his eyes and lay still on the bed, looking at the textured ceiling. He heard people in the kitchen getting their pie and coffee before starting the movie, and he got up and went downstairs to find Gaia.

"Honey, I'm realizing I should just fly out tonight instead of tomorrow. That way I can get settled in and rested before my meetings."

"I forget, where are you going?"

"Cayman."

"Nice."

"Yeah. Hopefully, I'll get to break away to enjoy it a bit. I'm working the whole time. The good news is there are some deep pockets there."

Gaia said quietly, "If you're going to leave me, I hope you wait until the kids are gone."

"What are you talking about?"

"I don't know. All these trips last minute…"

God, she was spot-on. Her intuition was perfect. But even though she was right, he felt indignant and amused at the accusation. "*What?* Listen, you're paranoid. Do you want to come with me and stay with me for a night or two? We'll have fun together when I'm not working, and you'll see there's nothing going on." Mark knew her answer before he asked.

"No," she said. "You know I can't. The kids have stuff. I need to get us ready to leave for my parents' when you get back next week."

"Yeah," he said. "That's right. We're all going to binghamton. Ok."

"Let me help you get ready."

"Thanks." God, she was so trusting and helpful. Gaia deserved a better man. He needed to become one. If he lost Gaia, he would lose any chance to find the good within himself.

"After you're packed, can you have dessert and watch some of the movie with the kids? They'd love to have you hang out with them before you go."

"Sure. Yeah. Great idea."

For a couple of hours, he sat with his family. He forced himself to ignore his negative thoughts. The pie and coffee were delicious and his kids were funny. He relaxed and smiled inside. Knowing he was leaving soon helped him better appreciate the final hours together. The movie was an old, stupid, comedy western with Jack Nicholson and John Belushi. He laughed and really enjoyed just *'being with'* as Gaia called it.

Why couldn't he feel like this all the time? Without the help of a drink or a xanax? Without knowing that he would be free of everyone in less than an hour? Soon, he'd be sitting in a leather airplane seat with a scotch in his hand and Sheila beside him – or bouncing on his lap – while they headed to the caribbean for relaxation and sunshine. He pushed all those questions out of his mind. There were too many to answer, and he wanted to focus on enjoying these last moments with Gaia and his children before he left.

Sitting there, he suddenly had a flashing insight of what his true purpose was – to be a devoted husband and father, faithful to his commitments. This was his last trip with Sheila, he decided. After this trip he was done chasing women, done chasing an urge that could never be fulfilled. Lust was an appetite that only increased the more it was fed, like a shark tasting the first drop of blood, transforming from a serene creature into a frenzied monster, devouring everything in its path and still never satisfied.

Goodbye family. Goodbye forever, he thought. *When I come home, I'll be a different person, a new man.* Their family trip to binghamton would be his rebirth. This was it. He'd wasted so much time, but at the end of this trip he would tell Sheila it was all over, and he would come home and make a fresh start. He would be true to Gaia for once – and forever.

And most of all, he realized, he would finally be true to himself.

TWELVE
incarceration

Man is free at the moment he wishes to be.
                                          – Voltaire

Excerpts from the textbook *Origin, Evolution, and Current Principles of the American No Law Movement, Fourth Edition,* by Sean McClusky.

Government Incarceration
No Law movement activists were infuriated by the enormous number of Americans imprisoned by the government. When the No Law movement began, the United States was the world's leading jailer. While the United States represented 4 percent of the world's population, it housed 25 percent of the world's prisoners. More than one of every one hundred American adults were in prison. One of every thirty-two citizens was under the supervision of the criminal justice system, including prison, probation, and parole. More than half the prisoners had been sentenced for nonviolent crimes, with an average sentence of more than fifteen years.

No Law leaders blamed the government for immoral abuses of power, including unreasonable drug sentencing laws, for-profit prisons run by corporations, felony disenfranchisement, and pay-to-stay programs.

Drug Sentencing Laws
The federal government's 'War on Drugs' was initiated in the 1970s and was pursued vigorously. Drug-law violations became the main driver of prison admissions for the next five decades. During this time, more people were put in prison for drug-law violations than for violent crimes. Figure 1a graphs the dramatic increase in the number of incarcerated Americans.

The War on Drugs contributed to the systemic mass incarceration of minorities, especially blacks. Minorities were more likely to be stopped, searched, arrested, convicted, harshly sentenced, and saddled with a lifelong criminal record.

figure 1a: Incarcerated Americans 1930–2020

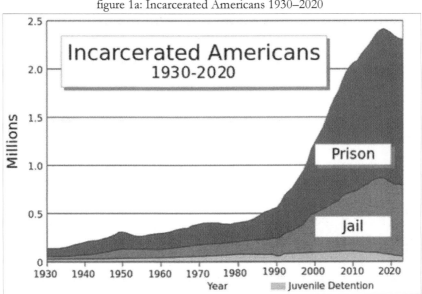

Prison Privatization

The 1980s saw the emergence of the for-profit prison industry. The for-profit prison industry became a major contributor to mass incarceration. Corporations operating prisons, such as the Corrections Corporation of America and the GEO Group, spent hundreds of millions of dollars lobbying the federal government, convincing lawmakers to expand the privatization of corrections facilities and to enact new statutes that increased incarceration, such as 'three-strike' laws.

Prison companies also signed contracts with the government that guaranteed prison beds would be filled. Most private prison contracts mandated that the government maintain a minimum occupancy rate – usually 90 percent – or the taxpayers had to pay for the empty beds. Some private prisons operated with a 100 percent occupancy guarantee.

Prison companies used their increasing profits from these quotas to lobby lawmakers for even more laws and tougher sentencing so that they could incarcerate even more citizens for even longer periods of time. This influence on the government by the private prison industry was referred to as the *prison–industrial complex*, a reference to President Dwight D.

Eisenhower's earlier warnings about the *military-industrial complex.*

No Law leadership proclaimed that for-profit prisons were counter to what should be the rehabilitative mission of the nation's criminal justice system. Instead, private prison contracts incentivized the government to keep prisons full. No Law leaders argued that the growing influence of the prison lobby commoditized human bodies in pursuit of profit. The influence of private prisons created a system that traded money for human freedom at the expense of the most vulnerable populations: minorities, immigrants, and the poor.

Felony Disenfranchisement

Felony disenfranchisement is the exclusion of citizens from voting after being convicted of a felony criminal offense. The United States was one of the most punitive nations in the world in denying felons the right to vote.

Punishment was not only meted out by the criminal justice system, but also perpetuated by policies denying child custody, voting rights, employment, business loans, licensing, student aid, public housing, and other public assistance to people with criminal convictions. Even if a person didn't face prison time, a drug conviction imposed a lifelong ban on many aspects of social, economic, and political life. Such exclusions created a permanent second-class status for millions of Americans, and this status fell disproportionately on people of color. Millions of voting-age minorities were denied the right to vote because of laws that disenfranchised people with felony convictions.

In the national election of 2024, over five million citizens were blocked from voting, up from one million in the 1970s. This comprised over 2 percent of potential voters and included 8 percent of African-American voters.

No Law proponents argued that disenfranchisement conflicted with the basic principles of democracy. It blocked those who were victims of the criminal justice system from having a voice in fixing it.

Pay-to-Stay Programs

A widespread practice in the United States, known as 'pay-to-stay', charged prison inmates a daily fee while they were incarcerated. The pay-to-stay charges were in addition to fines, restitution to victims, or any administrative costs incurred by going to court. For people in and out of prison – especially those struggling with drug addiction – this led to sky-high debts owed to the corporations that ran the prisons. People came out of jail with crippling debt.

No Law called for this practice to be eradicated, alleging that pay-to-stay debts devastated prisoners and their families, shifting insurmountable debt onto the poorest members of society who were already victims of the toughest criminal justice system in the world. No Law criticized the government for using law enforcement to generate revenue for private companies.

No Law Remonstrance

No Law leadership rallied followers to oppose the heavy-handedness and unfairness of the American criminal justice system. The group appealed to the growing number of Americans who were frustrated with a federal government that imprisoned and indebted its own citizens for the benefit of corporations, then left them disenfranchised and unable to participate democratically in changing the system. No Law leaders convinced a growing number of Americans that the only way to fix this problem was through a much more drastic course of action – peaceful overthrow of the American government.

THIRTEEN
homicide

But we were wise. We knew that man's heart, away from nature, becomes hard.
— Luther Standing Bear

As Sheila walked past him, Mark looked out at the crystal-blue caribbean sea beyond his balcony and listened to himself lie into the phone, "Hey hon, I'm just not going to make it back to the city from cayman for another couple days. There's a big deal here close to going through and I need to be here. I'm worried if I try to manage it remotely, it's going to fall apart."

"Hmm, ok," Gaia said.

"What do you want to do? Do you want to go ahead and drive to binghamton, and I can meet you there?"

"I was looking forward to driving with you. The kids really need time with you. Why don't I just call my parents and tell them we'll be there thursday instead of tomorrow. We'll stay in the city an extra couple days. If you fly back to kennedy thursday morning, we can pick you up at the airport and head to binghamton from there."

"Ok. I won't have all my stuff."

"I'll pack for you. Send me a text with what you want. If I forget anything, we'll run out."

"Yeah. Sorry."

"No problem. I love you."

Sheila walked past him again, and her amazing body, so young and firmly soft, distracted him. He wanted her again already, and he worried about her hearing him on the phone with Gaia, saying he loved her. But he also didn't really care, and maybe Sheila didn't really care either.

"Yeah. I love you too."

Mark put down the phone and sat still, looking out at the sea.

FOURTEEN
detonation

The temperature just before the detonation of the new york city atomic bombs was fifty-two degrees fahrenheit. Humidity was sixty-two percent. The wind was blowing north at two miles per hour. It was a sunny day in early may.

five... four...

three... two...

one...

and... hey...

how... long...

can...

a... moment...

pause...

forever.

...ignition...

All four atomic bombs detonated.

Gaia saw a flash.

New york city disappeared.

One… two… *skip a few*… eight million people… are gone… gone… *gone*.

Where do the souls go? We want to know!

Now, class, please plot the upper limit on how many people can die in a single moment.

Is there anything that is not allowed to happen?

FIFTEEN
confederacy

I prefer dangerous freedom over peaceful slavery.
— Thomas Jefferson

Griffin Turner sat on the small porch looking out at wilcox street. The july, chicago night was hot and humid, a slight breeze saved it from being stifling. He took another sip from a forty-ounce glass bottle. "I'm tired of buyin' lottery tickets," he said.

His girlfriend, Maggie, sat beside him in a blue fabric folding chair. "I hear you, Griff."

"We take a bunch of us. We take money and guns and we caravan to one of these No Law territories and we make our own enclave. I'm talkin' about acres, and we fence it in. And we show we can do it our way, without any government."

"Mmmmm," Maggie said.

"I'm a permanent outcast. I got federal felonies for drugs and guns and I can *never* escape that here. I look back at how *stupid* I was. I was groping in the dark. Now I see clearly. In No Law, I can start over and be the man I wanna be, instead of the man the government says I am. I can be born again. I can't do that anywhere else. No Law is the place."

"No Law's dangerous," Maggie said.

"Freedom's dangerous. You have to be willing to die for it. Picture it, babe. We'll see those rocky mountains, and it'll be a fresh start in a new world. There's no background checks. There's no pigs stoppin' you everywhere you go. We can do it our way. I'd rather die free than live as a slave, and that's what this government has turned us into – we're enslaved by handouts. At least, on the plantations, we had to work for a livin'. And anyway, *chicago's* dangerous. The big cities are being *wiped out* – new york, d.c. and l.a. in may – when more nukes come, we're gonna be next."

"But the feds aren't letting anyone in," Maggie said. "You've seen it. They've barricaded colorado. They might even shoot us if we try."

"The big checkpoints are surrounded by news guys. They won't shoot a bunch of black people on live tv – bad public relations. Anyways, *good*, let the pigs shoot. 'Cause we'll shoot back, and I guarantee we'll take out more of them than they will of us, 'cause we're fightin' for our freedom, while pigs are fightin' for a paycheck. The heart always beats the wallet. I believe that, baby. I *know* it. Just ask the vietcong, or the mujahedeen. The more I talk, the more I realize there's no choosin' it. I'm excited for the first time since I was seventeen because there's some hope, baby, that I can be a *man*. We'll make a new home, babe, where all of us can be born again. We'll be the saviors of all these men who are tired of being trained to be victims; tired of being animals caged in the ghetto behind bars of handouts."

"You think we could do it?"

"What's the alternative? Keep unzippin' uncle sam's pants? Look, maybe you have choices, Maggie, but I don't. I'm a free man with a life sentence, condemned to max out at minimum wage. I've stumbled, but I'm not stayin' down. I'm goin' to have a good life. I'm goin' to learn from every mistake I've ever made. Are you diggin' any of this?"

"Yeah. I'm hearin' you, Griff. But baby, we could get killed."

"Yeah, that could happen. You have a choice to make. I have no choice, but you do. You can stay here and make babies, and if you ain't nuked, you'll be housed and fed, educated and medicated – some medicaid prozac for you and some adderall for your kids. You'll get more benefits from the government if you stay single and make babies with no man around, you know how that works. The government's made brothers useless. A family lives better when the father abandons them. Our women and children get more handouts when there's no trace of their man around."

"Mmmmm."

"These projects all around chicago – every building is the government tellin' brothers 'we don't need you'. Big concrete middle fingers reachin' up to the sky. *You aren't needed, brother.* We can house your women and children – we'll feed them and clothe them and take care of them. *You aren't necessary, brother.* People think this subsidized housing is a hand up, but it's a shove down, back into the gutter."

"Givin' us a place to live is keepin' us down?"

"What do men do when no woman relies on 'em? They loaf, they drink too much, they look for trouble. Without responsibility forced on 'em by a woman, most men don't amount to much. Men are lazy and wild. Women motivate lazy men and tame the wild ones. Well, black women don't need black men 'cause it's all taken care of by the white men in feronia. They made it so our women are better off without us. She's more married to the government than her man."

"Hmmmm… maybe," Maggie said.

"But we need more freedom, not more money. You can't get everything. We live in a society where money is what people want, so they can't get freedom. I choose different. I choose freedom."

Maggie said, "But No Law territory is each man for himself."

"Listen, you think you're bein' *protected* by the law? I'm tellin' you, you're being kept down by it. The government enslaved us and then took credit for freein' us. The politicians wouldn't let us vote, but now they celebrate lettin' us. The law wouldn't let us in school with whites and then does us some big favor by lettin' us go where we *already* should have been. They step on our throats and then teach us to be thankful for cough drops. The government makes us poor, then trains us to be thankful for free crap housin' and free crap food and free crap educations and free crap healthcare. I'm done bein' thankful for government crap. If something can be given to you, then by definition, it can be taken away. I don't want anything given to me – respect, freedom, a job, money. I want it 'cause it's mine."

"You act like our lives are worse now than during slavery. We got problems, but it's better than slavery," Maggie said.

"Is it? At least slavery was *clearly* evil. Today what we have is a trick; millions of brothers trapped as slaves but fooled into *thinkin'* we're free. They've made us victims and victims are always slaves. We're enslaved by a government that says *nothin'* is our fault or responsibility. We're trapped in a life of poverty and lead-fortified drinkin' water and then we're perfectly trained to blame everyone else so we'll always stay on the plantation.

"The government gives us the two biggest lies of all – that someone *else* will look out for us, and that we should get respect without havin' to earn it. Listen to me, honey. I'm talkin' about us fightin' for ourselves, workin' for ourselves, with nothin' given to us. A few families with good men and plenty of weapons. We drive right in and set up our own place where we work for ourselves, and live for ourselves, and we have the freedom to kill anyone who gets in our way. We'll have our own true justice for once, not the fake justice of feronia that doles out a little truth here and there when necessary to quiet us down until we go back to killin' our own. I'm tired of waitin' for anyone else to do anything. Nobody can give me freedom. Nobody can give me equality or justice. If I'm a man, I take it because it's mine. You understand that?"

"Some of it. It's a lot to think about. I know we're held back. I'm not disagreeing with your diagnosis. I'm questioning your suggested treatment. I don't want to go to No Law. You got it wrong. It's dangerous there. We'd put our lives at risk goin' there. If you want to leave chicago, let's go somewhere without a bunch of out-of-control white people with guns."

"How could our lives be more at risk than they already are? We're imprisoned six times more than whites. One in three black men spends time in prison. Who's the law protectin'? When I go for a walk, I'm stopped by pigs with guns. When I drive, I'm pulled over by pigs with guns. You hear that helicopter? Hoverin' over our neighborhood right now? Look at those spotlights shinin' down from the sky – pigs flyin', searchin' for another black man to gun down. You're worried about white people with guns *there?* Hello? Look all around you, gorgeous."

Maggie chuckled, "I hear you."

"Dangerous? West wilcox street is dangerous. We're surrounded by killers, thugs, drugs – we're livin' in a war zone *now.* You think it can get any *worse* in No Law? It's more dangerous here in chicago. It's simmerin' and gettin' ready to boil over here and all across the country. It's ain't just black versus white. There's a clash between the oppressed and those who do the oppressing. The nukes in may were just the start. There's a war comin' between those who want freedom for everyone and those who want to continue the system of exploitation. The blasts in d.c., l.a., and new york are just the beginning of this war. Another thing is we got nothin', so who's goin' to come after us for anythin'? And we're black. We'll be surrounded by white people who're scared of *us*."

Maggie laughed.

"We're goin' someplace different. Someplace where we're runnin' our show. No government housin', no government education, no cops, no government food – no government nothin'. I mean, let's at least give it a try, right? It can't get any worse, babe, can it? I ain't got no job to lose. I'm already broke – I can't get no poorer. Nothin' bad can happen to us because all of it already has. So it's only up from here. I mean, really, the worst thing that could happen is we could die, and you're such a sweetheart that you're for sure goin' to heaven, so it wouldn't be that bad, right, gorgeous?"

Maggie laughed harder, her eyes glistening with floating tears. "Yeah baby, I love you. I love you so much."

"I got a plan. You come with me, and I'm gonna be king and you're gonna be queen. We'll have kids and they won't grow up slaves, trapped in this straightjacket. They'll think for themselves, with their own minds. You're goin' to be royalty, baby, so get ready."

"I love you, Griff. I'm scared, but I'll go with you." Maggie looked at him and smiled softly.

Griffin looked into her eyes. "That's my girl."

SIXTEEN
looping back

Mark Halberstam breathed in, then out. He felt a short whisper of a warm july breeze. Looking up, he saw a dusky, late evening sky. He tried to push the stupid fight with Sheila out of his mind. He needed to clear his head.

It was a quarter past eight in the evening. The red-orange sun was perched just above the adirondack mountains behind the lake. The water was almost still. Small ripples from hours ago, maybe yesterday, barely rolled across the glassy surface. He heard a seagull – once, twice. Farther away, a dog barked.

For some reason, he thought of Gabe Dismas, a friend from middle school. Gabe had been an outcast delinquent, an obnoxious maniac whom everyone else but him had ostracized. What happened to Gabe? Was he a still an outsider? Was he still alive? Maybe he'd died in one of the atombomb blasts.

He thought again of the argument with Sheila this morning and realized that he missed her. Sheila was all he had. It felt good to miss her, to miss something.

He sat down at a wooden picnic table and looked west, staring into the setting sun. *Maybe I'll go blind from staring right at the sun,* he thought, *and then I'll have an excuse to quit, to give up. I'll have no responsibilities. Blind people get a pass to be lazy. I'll finally be free. No one will rely on me.*

He'd left his work meetings early so he could sit and think before flying back to philadelphia. *I miss manhattan,* he thought. *It was everything I knew. New york city was my family, raising me, taking care of me, teaching me about myself and the world. I still don't believe it's gone. How can something real become unreal? Logically, things are permanent or temporary. Facts are permanent. A person, place, or thing is either real or it's an illusion. Maybe I'm innocent because I've only murdered illusions. Was Gaia an illusion? Were my kids? Was new york? If so, then I'm insane, and if I'm insane, then I'm innocent of murder by reason of insanity. Like an ignorant animal, the insane soul is uncontaminated by sin. Madness washes the soul clean.*

Since new york city, los angeles, and the district of columbia had been annihilated by atom bombs in may, he had to make frequent business trips to what Sheila called *'podunk land'* – small towns in upstate new york, vermont, maine, and new hampshire – places where wealthy people felt safer, places outside the next terrorist bullseye. The big cities were being abandoned by everyone who could afford to leave. Few thinking people wanted any part of the metropolises anymore; they wanted out of the gothams where millions could die in an instant flash.

Mark had relocated to philadelphia instead of podunk land. He moved to philly while almost everyone else with money was abandoning the big cities, leaving the poor behind. He needed the beating heart of a city, the juiced energy of millions of colliding ideas. He loved being amidst the urban hunt for money, power, and love. And part of him was perversely attracted to the threat of another terrorist atom bomb – dying in a blip, without even an instant of suffering. Everything would finally be over in a flick of white light.

He looked up from the red cracked paint on the picnic table and saw the sun had finally set. This far north, within fifty miles of the canadian border, the summer sun set later in the evening. The earth had twisted on its axis, never stopping, never pausing, making it appear that the sun had moved across the sky; and now another day was gone.

He looked at a flock of geese, or possibly ducks – the shapes were too far away to see which – sitting on the glowing water in the july dusk. *July.* His family died two months ago. This time last year they were alive. He was thirty-nine years old and what had he accomplished in his life? He was wealthier than ever. He'd travelled everywhere, bedded supermodels, made billions of dollars, and yet he'd done nothing significant except murder his entire family.

He thought about Jane from the meeting he'd left; she was a legal analyst on his team. He was almost certain that Jane would look stunning with her glasses off. Her smile was dazzling. Her luxurious brown hair and her powerful legs reminded him of Gaia. Gaia was always there in the back of his mind – *I do still love you, Gaia. I love you, I love you. I love you, Gaia. I love you, I love you.* He loved her more than ever – even though he'd betrayed her and killed her.

Jane, the legal analyst, wasn't slim, and that attracted him. He was increasingly turned off by the super-thin, hyper-fit, amphetamine-boned women that seemed to be everywhere. They were too flawless; they seemed artificial and mass-produced. He was done with stringy model types, for a while at least. He needed a woman with curves, a body that could comfort and nurture him.

No, he stopped himself. *No.*

No Jane tonight. No women tonight. The women – like the money, the cars, the homes, the booze, the trips – were just a way of hiding. Women were anesthesia. He had to stop sedating himself. He needed to diagnose problems and try to solve them, instead treating symptoms.

Jane was with a dozen other people in the meeting that he'd bolted from less than an hour ago. He was trying to buy an international cosmetics company, but the deal was stalled for two reasons. One, the seller was being completely unrealistic about the asking price. Two, almost all his employees were new; most of his people, and all the best ones, had died two months ago. His team's sloppiness infuriated him; he *hated* being unprepared. He'd sat in the meeting in a calm rage, wondering who he was going to fire.

Buying and selling companies was like dealing used cars. The game was the same, just the dollars and lies were bigger. Instead of tires, floor mats, and leather trim, they traded balance sheets, product lines, and people. The seller was trying to make his cosmetics company look reliable and racy, with plenty of miles still to be driven. Mark's team kicked the tires and looked under the hood, pointed out the worn treads and oil leaks, and pressured the seller to reduce the price. Mark's goal was to get a good deal on the business so he could flip it – detail the interior, patch the rust spots, apply a fresh coat of paint, and unload it later for a big profit.

After lunch, he sat through two plus hours of due diligence meetings and he suddenly became overwhelmed by all the phoniness, his and everyone else's. the fake smiles, the false projections, the feigned collaboration, the fawning optimism, layered on top of lies, layered on top of excrement. Everyone in the room was winning oscars, acting like they cared about anyone other than themselves. Corporate people – financiers, lawyers, bankers, executives, *himself* – were more heartless than murderers and rapists. Killers at least had human emotions – hate, rage, spite. Rapists burned with contempt, envy, and lust. In contrast, corporate people were inhuman androids, smiling robotic machines, human computers tallying up cash flows and asset values without any passion. Life's meaning was distilled into equations: earnings multiples, return on investment, debt to equity. Everything was profit or loss.

All existence came down to numbers on a spreadsheet – rows and columns that were pivoted and graphed to justify betrayal, pilfering, and exploitation. Every sin was washed cleaned by delivering a return to shareholders.

The spreadsheets used to excite him. The equations used to make him salivate. The numbers used to almost physically arouse him. But his sins had gone beyond greed in some perverse way that kept disturbing his soul. How much was too much? When was enough enough?

Last christmas, before the may blasts, his grandma had visited his oceanfront vacation mansion in the hamptons. Driving his grandma up the long driveway – past the stone walls, meticulous lawns, and manicured hedgerows – he'd kept sneaking looks at her. He wanted to see admiration in his grandmother's eyes, her appreciation of his incredible wealth.

"Do you like it, grandma?" he'd asked.

She turned and looked at him for a moment before she answered. "You can only be in one room at a time," she said.

"Yeah, thanks," he said.

At that moment, he'd thought she was proud, but weeks later her words came back to him. He'd gone back up to the ocean mansion in january to be alone, to get drunk for a few days by himself. The first night there he made the gigantic mistake of sleeping with his new twenty-something interior decorator – exactly what he had promised himself he would not do, no matter how tempted he was – but he did it like a lunatic.

After the girl was finally asleep, he'd gotten out of bed and walked through the entire mansion, lighting his way in the dark with his phone, walking alone through silent, unlived-in rooms where everything was perfectly furnished and untouched. In the dark, his grandmother's words came back to him.

You can only be in one room at a time.

He'd stood in an entryway between two adjoining rooms, one foot planted in each room. *You're wrong, grandma,* he thought, *I'm standing in two rooms at the same time you wrinkly, stupid, dying, nagging, jealous, old woman.* Then he'd stood still in front of a large window overlooking one of the topiary gardens. He looked out at the manicured landscape in the moonlight and saw drops that confused him, then realized he was crying.

You can only be in one room at a time.

Geese honked, waking him from his memory. Mark imagined that the geese were trying to tell him something. Who else were they trying to talk to? He was the only one here. He couldn't understand the geese, but he had a feeling that what they were saying was important. Geese didn't track appointments, deadlines, budgets, or profits. Which species was truly free? Which lived the more authentic life? The geese won hands down. They had something figured out, and they were trying to share the secret, but he couldn't understand them.

He looked at the lake and saw a man paddleboarding across the glassy water, a silhouette gliding in front the mountains, the pink dusk. *That guy is crazy*, Mark thought. It was almost dark and getting cold. But the man kept moving, surrounded by the honking geese that were louder now, all honking together. Their sound rose up and created a moment of cacophony. A leaf fell, tumbling and floating in a rhythmic dance on its way to the ground.

Ever since new york city disappeared, something had changed inside him. He didn't know what it was exactly, but the annihilation of his family and millions of other souls left ghosts that haunted his thoughts. Everything now seemed arbitrary, random, and pointless in a way that it hadn't before.

He sensed that everything was changing, looping back to some distant point in the past. There was less connectedness now. Collective thought was fading. The good of the group was being replaced with the freedom of the individual. Mankind was evolving backwards, unweaving and breaking the webs of interconnectedness that had been spun over centuries.

He'd been travelling too long. He'd been working too hard. He heard the sound of the geese fade away. They were done trying to talk to him. He was done listening. He was looking for something, but it wasn't here. Try to forget Jane, Gaia, Sheila, his children. Try to forget that he was a murderer. Try to forget that he hated himself.

He needed to get on the plane, get a drink in each hand, and get back to philadelphia.

SEVENTEEN
preproduction

Corby Myers, the award winning investigative journalist from the news program *Indicium*, felt nervous. He tried to force himself to sit still but kept fiddling with the pen and paper in front of him.

If this worked out, Corby would be the first journalist to interview Declan Kikas in more than three years. He looked over his pages of notes. Kikas, the founder of the No Law movement that was tearing apart america, occasionally posted essays online. In a post last year, Kikas wrote, "We're so far from truth. Our only hope to find it is pure, immaculate freedom. There is no map for uncharted wilderness, which means getting lost as we feel our way blindly through the maze. It means evolution, which means constant creative destruction."

In another post, Kikas wrote, "You worry too much about right and wrong. You worry too much about suffering and unfairness. In the true reality, there is no such thing as evil or inequity. Yes, in this world, this false reality within an illusion of time, there will be those things, and we can't avoid them. God is everything, and that means he's good *and* evil. God's a creator, and a cold-blooded killer. God comforts, and sadistically tortures. He came down to earth, and look at the example he lived. He had himself crucified, hung alive from a cross with metal spikes pounded through his hands and feet, his stomach sliced open, a crown of thorns pressed into his skull. God tortured then murdered himself. He asked himself for mercy, *'Father, if you are willing, take this cup from me,'* and he gave himself none."

And another post, "There is love in all of us. There is hate in all of us. There is mercy and there is punishment. There is forgiveness and revenge. And there is always increasing wisdom."

Corby thought about his conference call that morning with the network

83

executives who were skittish about his interview with america's public enemy number one. It was a tough sell, but the key was to talk dollars. Executives rose to the top by selling their souls in increments. It wasn't a question of principles; it was a question of how much money could be made.

"Tim, Tim, listen! It's only july. Tons of time to sell this in before september. If you promote this heavy in august we'll hit seventy awareness the week before. By day before we'll be ninety... by sunday morning, only drunken, homeless morons won't know. We'll decimate everything else. Jess, hello! Anybody home? Right after the football game! The game's just sucked like always, and they wanna see this guy Kikas. What makes him dangerous? Is he like me? Listen, Bill, this will be the most talked about event in television history. Don't listen to Jim! Talk to Don! If I take this somewhere else, I'll eat you alive. You'll be cleaning out hamster cages for a living. You better believe me! 'Cause I'm out unless, unless yeah, you know, at least three mill, maybe four we're talkin' now. Well, should've signed me a month ago. CNN will offer a lot more. Right, yeah. Right."

He looked over at Luke, his producer, another sceptic who still had to be convinced. "This will make your career," Corby said.

"Corby, he's a terrorist."

"*Alleged* terrorist."

"You're giving a terrorist a podium to speak from. He's a fugitive who's been sentenced to death. You're letting him rationalize national rebellion. You're an accomplice to a traitor."

"Look, everything we see about the guy is a hash of mainstream media slice and dice – snaps of scowls and snips of sneering words. They've turned him into a comic-book villain. But it's not that simple. Millions of people support him; they voted in No Law in colorado and oregon, so some part of his message makes sense to some people. I'm not saying that he's *right*. I'm not saying that I *agree*. I'm saying that we need to be able to *understand* him if we want to make our own decisions – and especially if we want to fight him."

"Declan Kikas wants to destroy our country. He's a criminal. He's evil."

"Careful with your vocabulary. Being a criminal isn't the same as being evil. Talk to Gandhi or Christ or Nelson Mandela about that. Truth to power. And anyway, I'm not saying he's good. I'm simply being a *journalist* – remember that word? Before we cared about ratings and bonus checks and sponsors? I'm simply giving the american people – the whole world – a chance to hear his point of view."

"Journalism's dead, decomposing for decades. It's all show business."

"You're making my point, Luke. Look, it'll either be brilliant journalism or genius show business. It's *both*. We're bringing truth to the public *and* we're going to have the most highly rated, most watched interview in the world – with your big fat producer credit colliding into the eyeballs of billions of viewers. If *that* doesn't get you a hot date, then nothing will."

Luke laughed, "Hey man, if I can get a hot date – who isn't insane – then I'll *join* Declan Kikas and his merry band of american maniacs. Women are attracted to outlaws, right? Maybe that could be my new thing, my new style – *outlaw producer*. There's probably a whole look that goes with that – no tie, buttons undone on my shirt. I wish I could get some chest hair – not a forest, but more than two or three weeds." Luke looked down at his chest.

Corby chuckled, "Way off topic, my friend. Back to now. Let's get prepared. I want to review the latest drafts of questions. I want to go through the storyboards and shot locations for the whole day with Kikas – definitely want shots in and around the No Law perimeter, shots of the feds outside the fence and the No Law vigilantes inside it. There needs to be lots of guns – from both sides. I want some supporting interviews with folks inside colorado and some of the few who are authorized to travel across the border. I think there's enough material that we could sell this to the network as a two- or maybe even three-night special – two hours each night. We run promotions across the entire network for two weeks leading in, use tons of material for the promos without coming close to giving it all away."

"No way, Corby. I mean, maybe *one* two-hour special. Two nights is too much politics. It gets boring. You're overestimating people's attention span."

"*Come on!* The republic is fracturing apart and No Law is the hammer pounding it into pieces. Of course people care!"

"Nope, no one really cares. We need some other spin. Are there any celebrities who live in the No Law states? Or who've been there? Or even support them in some way? If we get a famous actress who's part of the story, it could really help. Maybe Liz Jakim? I think she's from colorado. We could interview her about being from the first state that's gone completely No Law."

"God, that's *genius*, Luke. And she must have some new movie coming out."

"Yep. Exactly. Right. So she can promote her latest project. There must be at least three or four other celebrities from colorado, oregon, or idaho we can include that will up the buzz."

"Idaho?"

"They aren't official yet, but the latest polls indicate No Law will easily pass there in November. If we have some celebrities as part of this, it'll be huge – grab one for each key demographic – whites, blacks, teens, spics, etcetera."

"*God yes*. Yes! Yes! Yes! I love it. This is *genius*."

"Thanks. I'll put someone on it – we'll come up with the long list and start contacting agents to see who we get. Many of 'em will love it, a great way to get promotion within the lens of a serious piece, not just another ten minutes on a late-show couch."

"Ok, yeah. And share that plan with the network so they can start finding us a three-night slot – we can easily do that, and we'll have the whole country glued in for three nights in a row!"

"Well, the network will be worried about finding sponsors. They're gonna have a tough job selling spots with all the controversy around Kikas. It's too much. I mean, this guy is an enemy of the government, a fugitive. People are gonna be outraged, saying you shouldn't be interviewing him, you should help the government catch him instead."

"I disagree. The advertisers aren't sponsoring Kikas. They're sponsoring '*Indicium*' – the longest-running, highest-rated, investigative program on the planet. We handle topics that are controversial – that's why everyone watches us, and if they want to sell more shampoo, beer, and boner pills, then they need to pay big-time. It's *television*. They're trying to sell crap, not elevate mankind. Look, the response to the critics is we're on their side, we're all fighting against the terrorists that are tearing our country apart, and part of that war is exposing the terrorists' message for what it is, to let these criminals show themselves for who they are, instead of hiding behind their propaganda and slogans."

"Ok."

"You need to push for exclusivity – minimal advertising breaks sold at a huge premium. Make the advertisers pay more to join an exclusive club – a couple breaks, four at most every hour, and charge through the roof for every spot 'cause *everyone* will watch this – we're going to be living with the guy for almost an entire day, on the move with him, seeing his home, his nutso followers, his work with his leadership team. People either love this guy, and they're going to watch, or they hate him and they'll watch. Everyone will watch. Also, there are at least a couple spots for product placement – it needs to be authentic – but we can have a soda can on the interview table or a bag of chips on a dashboard. We drive around in jeep or a suburban, depending on who's on board."

"Yep. Good. It's on the list."

"Thanks, Luke. This is going to be *huge*."

EIGHTEEN
embargo

THE FERONIA MESSENGER

Feds Tighten Colorado and Oregon Blockades
Colorado President Calls Sanctions an "Act of War"

BY JOSEPH BURSTIN

FERONIA – President Peter Scott today ordered tightened enforcement of the two-month-old blockade encircling the No Law republics of Colorado and Oregon, and he pledged his support for pro-Feronia opposition groups.

In a statement issued before the upcoming No Law vote in Idaho, Scott said the trade and travel sanctions against the two former American states were not just a policy tool but a "moral statement."

"Ever since the terrorist nuclear attacks destroyed Los Angeles, New York City, and our former capital, we've been fighting enemies from outside our country," Scott said. "Now, the No Law terrorists are trying to destroy us from within. Four months ago, Coloradans used the ballot box to eliminate all federal laws, followed by Oregon. The tyranny of liberty that rules Colorado and Oregon cannot go unpunished and must not spread," Scott said. "The United States stands opposed to No Law, and we will continue to tighten sanctions against the Colorado and Oregon regimes until they hold democratic elections that repeal No Law and recognize federal authority."

Richard Johnson, President of the Republic of Colorado, issued a statement saying, "The federal government is ignoring the will of the people. Sanctions are an act of war. We want to live in peace and be left alone. We won't start a fight, but if they insist on starving our children with blockades, then we will fight in self-defense. This fight for freedom demands all our strength. Resisting the federal government requires every Coloradan to stand strong. If victorious, we have everything to hope for. If defeated, we have nothing left to live for."

President Scott's actions have also angered Canada, Mexico, and a number of nations that issued statements opposing the measures, highlighting the negative impacts on trade. The Japanese and UK prime ministers issued a joint statement sharply condemning the sanctions and highlighted the naval blockade of Oregon as an excessive reach of U.S. power.

Despite efforts by some lawmakers to allow food and medicine sales, President Scott has vowed to oppose any effort to weaken the sanctions. Scott said he's ordered both Homeland Security and the Defense Department to add ships to the Oregon naval blockade, increase ground patrols, and conduct more aerial surveillance. Scott also ordered additional funding for federal government organizations that are working with pro-Feronia groups in both states.

"We must uphold the law. We need to enforce limits on these rogue states while ensuring support can reach the pro-federal activists inside them," Scott said. "We will oppose every state that abandons the restraints that unite us as Americans."

Joseph Burstin can be reached at burstin@newyorkmessenger.com

NINETEEN
pow wow

Hear me, people: We have now to deal with another race – small and feeble when our fathers first met them, but now great and overbearing. The love of possession is a disease with them. These people have many rules that the rich may break but the poor may not. They take their tithes from the poor and weak to support the rich and those who rule.
— Sitting Bull

It's a warm, august evening in a field outside blackfoot, idaho. Thousands of people are gathered in front of a makeshift stage. Cars, tents, and campers are circled outside the crowd. A large banner above the stage reads, "NO LAW RALLY! VOTE FOR FREEDOM! VOTE FOR IDAHO ON NOVEMBER 5TH!"

The man standing alone on the stage has a three-day beard and blue eyes. Sharp angles outline his profile, and his face is a mask of lines; each line maps a journey, and each journey is a story. The lines tell stories of misery and solace, of heartache and love, of betrayal and loyalty, of despair and laughter, of mistakes and learning, of wisdom earned.

The man steps up to the microphone, he looks out across the clusters of men, women, and children. Some dogs roam and weave through the crowd, tails wagging. A family catches his eye for a moment: a father wearing a flannel shirt, a mother close beside him with an infant in her arms, two small children, a boy and a girl, lean into her faded blue jeans, all of them look up at him on the stage. He stands up straight and says:

Ladies and gentlemen, my name is Charlie Kristopher. I wish I could say it's great to be here, but the truth is I have no desire to be here. I want to be home. I want to be with my family, my animals, my neighbors, and my gardens. I want to be fishing. I want to live a simple life of freedom, hard work, and self-reliance. I don't like speeches. I don't like people who give them. And yet, I'm here in front of you.

My philosophy has always been to live and let live. I don't want to convince anyone of anything.

But come, let us reason together.

I have to be here.

I'm here for the No Law movement and I'm asking you to support the repeal of all federal laws on november fifth.

I'm here because I'm tired. We are all tired – we're all exhausted by the laws that restrict our freedom, that imprison us, that force us to live how others want us to live. We are tired of the laws that support the lazy, the corporations, the politicians, the lawyers. We are tired of the laws that burden the hardworking. We are tired of the laws that protect imaginary corporations at the expense of real people.

We are surrounded by parasites. Below us are the lazy masses demanding we pay for their food, shelter, education, and healthcare. Above us are the rich corporations who exploit us. Wall street makes nothing! Creates nothing! Provides nothing! And yet wall street gets richer and richer at our expense. Politicians, wall streeters, lawyers, bankers – they produce nothing, but these parasites write the laws that let them latch on and take more and more from all of us.

A few cheers of agreement rose up. The crowd seemed larger now. Charlie felt them listen. He felt them hunger for someone to say something true, and he felt from all of them a prayer that maybe tonight they would hear truth. He pushed his palms flat against his shaking legs and he continued:

The terrorist attacks in may prove that the federal government can't even protect our country. Our leaders have done exactly the opposite. By meddling continuously overseas for decades, they've made the world hate us. In our name, with our dollars and our children, our government has bombed, killed, tortured, and oppressed people all around the world. The world hates us and wants to kill us, just like we would hate them if they came here and built bases across our countryside; or patrolled our towns with their tanks; or cruised their warships along our coasts; or if they flew their warplanes, attack helicopters, and drones over our neighborhoods.

The federal government is supposed to keep us safe, but instead, it's made the world hate us. That hate led to the terrorist nuclear attacks, and now over ten million americans from new york city, los angeles, and the district of columbia are dead. Millions more are poisoned and dying slowly from radiation. This is all the result of federal government meddling.

When will it end? It won't end until we put a stop to it. Centralized government is an evil we no longer need!

We need more freedom – freedom from the perpetual wars and foreign meddling that provoke terrorists to attack us, and freedom from the federal government sticking its nose in our local workplaces, bedrooms, hospital rooms, classrooms, and checkbooks.

We are done with the lobbyists, the career politicians, and men with the arrogance, greed, and stupidity to think they can tell four hundred million souls how to live their lives. We're tired of the laws that pervert the natural order that god has created. Why must the working masses suffer while the lazy and well-connected cackle all around them?

A single, soft cry of "Yeah!" came from the crowd, and Charlie spotted the glow of a small campfire on the perimeter. The firelight flickered through the shifting bodies. Charlie felt some of his nervousness leave him, he could feel that his words were connecting. He pushed his hair back off his forehead and said:

The incarceration rate of the united states is the highest in the world. We're four percent of the world's people, but we lock up twenty-five percent of the world's prisoners. We have seventy percent of the world's lawyers. Lawyers are not needed when honest men speak plainly with each other. We don't need lobbyists and corporations making laws to imprison our family and neighbors.

My friends, idahoans are fearless. We are brave. We are not scared of liberty; we are not scared of the truth. And we will prevail. We will make idaho a free nation in november. And if we don't prevail this november, then we will prevail the november after that, or the november after that, or the november after that! Because there is no uncertainty about reaching our destination. There is only a question of how soon we will arrive there. We will repeal all federal laws.

In the first two states where we've been successful – colorado and oregon – they've put fences around us. They've stopped everything from coming in and going out. That's fine. The fences, soldiers, and guns expose our opponents for who they truly are, and those fences will come down when every state is a No Law nation, when every state is free.

In colorado and oregon, at first, the feds tried to move in and take over, but they couldn't outnumber us. So far, they've been reluctant to attack and murder their own citizens, for then the truth would be apparent for all to see. So they've backed off to the perimeters, thinking that they can fence freedom in. But in time, those fences will come down.

Ask yourself: Why does anyone oppose the idea of local government? Why do men who preach the rule of law oppose our freedom to choose the laws we want to live by? The No Law movement is a peaceful rebellion. We are winning our liberty from the federal government at the ballot box, through free and open elections, not force.

Our federal government preaches the rule of law, laws passed thousands of miles away by a few hundred old men who stay in power by begging corporations for money. But we preach the rule of freedom and justice – the rule of each person, of our family, of our neighbors, of our community. God gave us only ten commandments, and yet our government has given us thousands of volumes of tangled statutes that make every one of us a criminal. There are libraries of laws you couldn't read in a lifetime, so how can you comply with them? We are all criminals under federal law. It's unnatural. What is natural is the rule of the individual, the rule of the human heart and mind.

Support the repeal of all federal laws on november fifth! Support liberty and freedom. I call upon the motto of new hampshire, the motto that proclaims the truth and the destiny that's written into all our hearts, "Live free or die!"

A voice yelled from the crowd, "Live free or die!" Another voice jammed in, shouting, "No Law!" Charlie continued:

Every man is born naked. He's not born carrying law books. He's not born wearing judge's robes or the suit and tie of a wall street thief. He's not born with a pen in his hand for dotting i's and crossing t's on page after page of intricate paperwork just so that he can build a home, work, travel, go to school, or see a doctor. Man is born with his conscience written into his heart, and that is all he needs. Everything else comes from thieves and liars who want power over you, who want to siphon off your livelihood one percentage point at a time. Every man is born free.

We will be liberated once and for all, as nature intended, as our founding fathers intended. We will be governed by the conscience within our hearts and the wisdom of our families and our neighbors, instead of living under laws imposed on us by corporations, lobbyists, and self-serving politicians. They won't control us any longer because there will be no laws to entrap us, there will be no laws by which to imprison us, there will be no laws by which they can enslave us.

Until the day when idaho is free, I'm asking you to work harder. We must! We must all work harder. And soon we will win.

And now the crowd was quiet. Their minds collectively opened, their mouths collectively silent. The words that needed to be said by all of them were being said by the old, honest man alone on the stage. Charlie watched a small bug fly across his vision. People were harder to see now that it was dark, but he could feel them, their understanding and desire for freedom was flowing and the energy touched him, sparking him to raise his voice for his conclusion, putting an arm in the air while he spoke:

There is no question that the No Law revolution will be victorious. The only uncertainty is how long our journey will be. The harder we work, the sooner we will reach our destination. Every hour we work is another step closer to No Law. We will get there. We will overcome every obstacle.

We, who are pushing the No Law movement forward, we see the future clearly. You, who fight against us, you are living in the past, a past world where the rich and powerful corrupted the law to serve themselves, a past world where small numbers of powerful people used the law to imprison and entrap the majority, a past world where piles of books and words bound mankind into slavery.

No more.

Brothers and sisters in the No Law movement, stand together all across this great state. We will return to where we began – Wild and free, liberty! Wild and free, liberty! Wild and free, liberty!

No Law! No Law! No Law!

Charlie raised both his arms in the air with his last words and stepped back from the podium. It was dark now except for strands of solar lights strung across the stage. The crowd cheered and joined the chant, "No Law! No Law! No Law! No Law!..."

TWENTY
lassitude

Like a man who has been dying for many days, a man in your city is numb to the stench.
— Chief Seattle

Mark Halberstam got back to his apartment in philadelphia before eight on a friday night in august. He sat on the couch with a drink *(My fifth? Or sixth?* he asked himself) and listened to Sheila's latest rant.

"These people are *rednecks*. They're worse than rednecks – they're apes who take *pride* in being stupid."

God, does she ever stop whining? Mark wondered. *But she's right.* Aspirational city leaders had started calling philly the "new new york". *If* there could ever be another new york, philadelphia *maybe* had the best chance. *Maybe someday.* But philadelphia was still too hickish, too rough around the edges. For now, future aspirations only highlighted present inadequacies.

"You're a manhattan snob," Mark said.

"Ha," she laughed. "Yeah, I learned that from you."

"Well, we can't be snobs now. Everything's gone."

"Do you ever feel like we should be sadder than we are?" she asked.

"Yeah. And more grateful. The god I'm not sure I even believe in picked *us* to be saved. It's a miracle that we're alive. We're supposed to be dead. We were supposed to be in the city."

"I guess not," Sheila said.

"Yeah. Or are we dead? Maybe we're ghosts."

"Why would we be in philly? There's a lot of other places we could float to, or fly to."

"Haunt. Let's get dressed up, go out for a nice dinner, act rich," he said.

"We *are* rich," she told him, "so it's no fun acting. What do you want to do? Go *clubbing*? Let's cuddle here. I just want to be with you."

We're rich? Mark thought. No honey – *I'm* rich, not *you*. You're just good-looking. That's it. You've got what money can't buy – youth. But in ten years – newsflash – you'll have nothing.

Mark looked into his glass. "I need to do something."

"I'm sorry if you think cuddling with me is boring."

"I wonder if god gets bored. God must be bored out of his mind, right? He's experienced everything, otherwise he's not god."

"I'm not sure," Sheila said.

"*That's* an understatement. Anyway, I want to do something besides sit around here. It's the first day of the rest of my life," he said.

"Yeah. So don't screw it up."

God, how did all this happen? he thought. *Who is Sheila? I once thought she was smart and witty, but I was just blinded by her dazzling attractiveness. She's a repository of prerecorded repartee. She's a library of well-rehearsed reactions that she's carefully archived so they can be retrieved quickly enough to appear as wit. There's little intelligence; there's no creativity. I was blinded by her beauty, by her body, by my lust. Only a blind man can truly love a beautiful woman because only a blind man can treat her honestly. Every seeing man is stupefied by female beauty. I'm sorry, Gaia. I should have died with you. I should have been there with you and our children. Our souls should be somewhere together for eternity, or nowhere together for oblivion.*

How could one small, selfish decision follow him the rest of his life? What could he do to repent for an unforgivable sin? The bible said an eye for an eye, a life for a life. But he only had one life to give – his own – in exchange for killing his wife and four children. Could suicide be good karma? At least a step towards atonement? Maybe his death could pay the debt he owed for murdering his family with his lust and lies. *I need another drink right now.* He reached over to the bottle of canadian whisky and poured more into his glass.

Maybe killing himself was the right call. Maybe suicide could save his soul. There was a cabinet of guns in the office. He imagined going in there, loading a beretta, turning on music, and waltzing in slow circles with the black weapon, kissing it and caressing it before he put the barrel next to his skull, said a final, faithless prayer, and pulled the trigger. Would suicide condemn him to eternal oblivion? Or damnation? Would it cancel his sins and put him back with Gaia? God, if he could just see her and tell her he was so sorry. *Why did I change my mind? Why? Why? Why? Why?* The smallest, most unimportant decisions mattered the most. The flick of a piece of dust could change an entire universe. One moment of lust had cursed him, destroyed his world and his fate, made him a murderer forever.

He had to get Gaia out of his head, but he couldn't. Her ghost hovered there with her love and loyalty – damning him; his betrayal haunted him everywhere. He should run away from everything and start fresh. A verse from the bible came to him, something about having to be born again to be a child of god. He'd always been confused by the passage; how could anyone be born again? But maybe now he knew what Jesus meant. He should start over. Leave work, the lawsuits, and all the disputed assets behind – take off for a shack in one of the No Law states. His life was a mess. He was disoriented behind the wheel going ninety miles an hour; he needed to pull off the highway before he crashed.

He realized Sheila was talking and tried to listen.

"...and I feel like you're not happy and blaming things on me. But look, I don't owe you anything or have responsibility – you screwed this up yourself. I mean, if anything it's only because of me that we're alive. If it wasn't for me, you'd be dead with your family. But I keep feeling like you think *I* did something wrong."

"Yeah."

"I need to hear you say that."

"What?"

"Say, 'I screwed this up myself.'"

"I screwed this up myself," Mark said, staring out through the floor-to-ceiling apartment window, across the philadelphia skyline, then looking down at the whisky in his glass. He didn't remember even making himself a drink. The flight home this evening already seemed a lifetime ago, or maybe it was a dream?

"I screwed this up myself," he said again.

She laughed. "Mark, honey, are you ok?"

"No."

"I can tell."

"Do you want to go out?" he asked. "I'm going out tonight, and I'm fine alone if you want to stay in." *I'm better if I'm alone,* he thought. *I need to be free from dealing with anyone else's perspectives.*

"I'm *not* going out tonight."

"Ok," he said, wondering if Sheila had taken any pills. Probably. She was confident and relaxed. He wondered which ones and how many she took.

::<>::<>::<>::<>::<>::<>::<>::<>::<>::

An hour later, Mark Halberstam was sitting at a varnished wooden restaurant bar; in front of him was a plate with steak, salmon, and asparagus. He had a pilsener glass of beer, a tumbler half full of balvenie scotch on the rocks, and an untouched glass of water.

Work. He should check in with his team to see if they needed anything, but work was driving him insane. Every project was behind schedule, every deadline missed. Everyone disliked him. He'd told everyone to work late, to come in early, to put in nights and weekends without whining if they still wanted to have a job – unrealistic expectations they could never meet. *Nice leader. I'm supposed to set the example – the first to arrive and the last to leave. But I simply can't work a moment more today.*

A loud voice spoke behind him, "Our next act is all the way from the green mountains of vermont! Please put it together for Justin LaPointe!"

He turned and watched a young, shaggy-haired man step onto the small stage in the corner. Justin LaPointe didn't acknowledge the crowd. He simply took a seat on a wooden stool and fiddled with plugging in his beat-up, acoustic-electric guitar, then adjusted the microphone stand. His guitar was brown, scratched, unvarnished wood. The kid wore an unbuttoned flannel shirt, under which he saw a white t-shirt with a picture of an eagle and the words "No Law" emblazoned across it.

A "No Law" nut, Mark thought. I thought the No Law maniacs were out west, but now these people are in the northeast. The crazy idea was spreading. The feds needed to get some control over this No Law thing before it spiraled into total chaos.

The kid started strumming, then sang out in a voice that carried, filling up the restaurant. His music and lyrics became everything:

I'm closing up shop, selling off my store
I know this city doesn't need me no more
I know it ain't no mystery
I'm going on back to bear country

My back is broke, my head is numb,
this new generation makes me feel old and dumb
the road is dark, but I can see
I know I'm getting close to bear country

The city was killing me, now I know
it was hurting, it was taking its toll
it'll take my body, it'll never take my soul
it'll take my body, it'll never take my soul
it'll take my body, it'll never take my soul

The chord progressions cast a spell that took Mark outside time, then he fell back down into the lyrics and realized that the kid was still singing, his tousled hair falling around his face:

And I will walk till I fall to my knees
until my heart stops, until it starts to bleed
my heart will always be in bear country
my heart will always be in bear country

The city was killing me now I know
it was hurting, it was taking its toll

it'll take my body, it'll never take my soul
it'll take my body, it'll never take my soul
it'll take my body, it'll never take my soul

The words gripped him. He'd never met Justin LaPointe, but this kid was singing to him and he needed to understand. Where was bear country? What exactly was this kid singing about? Was it the No Law territories? The *outlaw territories*, he'd heard a radio host call them. The two No Law states hadn't seceded from the union, there hadn't been a formal civil war, but they'd stopped taking any assistance from the government. They'd closed down all federal agencies, military bases, and courthouses, and they were only ruled now by local governments: state law still existed in oregon, county law only in colorado. It was crazy in colorado – one county had a speed limit, another didn't. One county allowed hard drugs, another didn't. One county had socialized healthcare, another didn't.

He was confused. He felt tired and stupid. Why? *Why?* Why was he still trying? What was he even trying for? He needed a change. He needed to get away from his whole life and start over from scratch.

When he'd flown back to philly that evening, he'd asked his pilot to fly over manhattan, and his pilot was brave enough to do it. The airspace over all five boroughs was officially a no-fly zone, with a file-mile perimeter due to excessive radiation, but this wasn't actively enforced. There was no risk of being shot down or anything, just the health risk that came with flying over the nuclear contamination – probably the equivalent of smoking twenty packs of cigarettes. Screw it – he didn't want to live any longer than he had to. He wanted to see the world's largest ghost town again.

"We're approaching, Mr. Halberstam," the pilot said over the intercom. "Look out at three o'clock. I'll take us right over the western side of manhattan – not that you'll recognize it. It's nothing now but a stew of hot, wet ashes."

He put in his earbuds and listened to an album by Evangelos Odysseas Papathanassiou called *"1492: Conquest of Paradise"*. The music had no lyrics, but it had meaning beyond words. The music brought a new perspective to the rubble below. It was amazing. Everything he'd thought was so important, everything he'd dreamed about being king of, was gone. Parts of manhattan were still on fire and smoldering even now in august, more than three months later. The flattened ashes were so poisonous that he was taking days off his life by flying a thousand feet above them.

Looking at the smoking landscape below him, Mark thought, *Paradise has been conquered. We did it.* We came, we saw, we conquered. There was some death wish inside man that wasn't happy with just paradise; he had to improve on it and make it better until finally it was a perfect pile of ashes.

The ruins below seemed holy in some way. *I'm the only man alive looking down upon millions of dead souls. I'm an angel floating above the largest graveyard in the universe. Instead of wings on my back and a harp in my arms, I'm in a gulfstream jet, listening to music on my phone.*

He thought back to may. Manhattan disappeared. Then, a few days later, the district of columbia, then a day after that, los angeles. N.y.c, d.c., l.a.: *the annihilated acronyms.* Gone, gone, and *gone.* Kaboom, kaboom, *kaboom...*

The nuclear attacks on the district of columbia occurred during a joint session of congress while the president was addressing the nation about the new york attacks. Almost the entire united states government disappeared during the nationally televised broadcast – the president, vice president, speaker of the house, the supreme court, and almost every congressman and senator. It would have been an unbelievable scene in a novel, except it was real. On the television screen, it was a blip, then static, then the federal government was gone.

Los angeles was obliterated the next day by three atomic blasts. After los angeles, america was knocked down to her knees – like a barely conscious boxer tangled up in rubber ropes, unsure where the blows were coming from or why he was even in the ring. *America should arguably have been saner after everyone in los angeles died,* Mark thought. But that hadn't happened. Los angeles crumbling into the pacific had sealed the deal, a brick dropped onto an already teetering scale. The country tilted into craziness.

Now, more than three months later, the federal bureaucracy was still incapacitated, but things were starting to stabilize; the chaos appeared to have bottomed out. The government was slowly firing back up. The country had a new president – following the constitutional lines of succession, the secretary of agriculture, who had been in idaho during the nuclear attacks, was now president. New senators and representatives had been quickly elected.

Last month, congress passed a law that for the next three years, the nation's provisional capital, named *feronia*, would rotate monthly amongst twelve cities: boston, philadelphia, cleveland, atlanta, chicago, saint louis, minneapolis, kansas city, dallas, miami, seattle, and san francisco. Every state had to keep one senator and one representative physically outside feronia, participating remotely via video conference, so if (*when?* Mark thought) feronia was attacked, a full delegation of politicians would survive.

The emerging federal government was struggling. There were big problems: finding and fighting unknown nuclear terrorists and controlling pockets of rural america that were increasingly getting out of control. The No Law legislation had passed in colorado and oregon, and there were a growing number of other enclaves that now governed themselves completely separate from state and federal laws – amish, mormons, white supremacists, and islamic fundamentalists were just some of the groups that were calling their own shots in different parts of the country.

Everything was going crazy. The country was falling apart.

Mark noticed both his glasses of alcohol were empty. He ordered another round of drinks and studied his reflection in the mirror behind the bar.

::<>::<>::<>::<>::<>::<>::<>::<>::<>::

By the time Mark got home, it was after midnight. Sheila was in bed but still awake, lying on her side, her gorgeous face illuminated in the pitch-black room by the glow of her phone screen. He wanted to be with her, but he didn't want to ask or hint; he wanted her to put down the stupid phone, turn to him, and ask him to come to her. But she just stared at the screen.

He said, "I should do some work before I go to bed."

"Ok," she said, not looking up from her phone.

He took off his suit and put on his pajama bottoms, moccasin slippers, and a long-sleeved grey t-shirt. "What are you doing on that thing?" he asked.

She waited before finally answering, "Looking at stuff."

He wanted to rip the phone out of her hands and throw it into the wall. Instead, he asked, "What stuff?"

She waited longer to answer this time. *To annoy him? To make something up? Because she was scared he'd get mad at her?* "About fibroids," she said.

"Oh," he said. She was constantly scanning the internet for illnesses that she, or her mom, or sister, or him, or someone she knew, might have. She was very interested in illness and in the weather, which struck him as the curiosities of an uncreative, unintelligent mind. *She's almost stupid,* he thought. *Her only serious contemplations are around dinner plans, vacation destinations, and what to wear. I made a mistake falling for her. I guess that's my fault, not hers.*

He walked into his office, logged onto his computer, and found dozens of messages from his team filling his email inbox. He turned away from the screen, stood up, and studied the gun cabinet. Each weapon sat still, waiting for him to choose it, pick it up, hold it, load it, and pull its trigger. Then he looked out his office window, contemplating the lights of the philadelphia skyline.

Something had to change. He had to find something inside himself that he could love. He had to become someone different than he was. How could he love anyone or anything if he couldn't love himself? He had to find some way to start over, to put his past behind him.

He stared at the rows of guns and knew one thing, his life had to be different, soon.

TWENTY TWO
transcript

Partial transcript from C-SPAN's program *Feronia Journal* with host Jason Myrtle. This transcript was compiled from corrected closed captioning.

Host: And we end C-SPAN's *Feronia Journal* with open phones. We're live from August's Feronia, Cleveland, Ohio. Any political or policy issue you want to talk about. If you want to talk about campaign finance reform, the war on domestic terrorism, the No Law movement, or current congressional races, the phone lines are yours. The number is two-zero-two, seven-four-eight, eight thousand. Uh, you can start calling in. The phones are open. First caller, Ramona from Sidney, Nebraska. You are first. Good morning. Hi.

Caller: Yeah. Thanks for taking my call. You know, one big problem I have with how the federal government is handling this No Law thing is they seem powerless against it. I live here near the border of Colorado. I mean, I understand that ever since New York got destroyed, and L.A. and D.C., they're still trying, you know, to hold the terrorists accountable and fight this war overseas against the terrorists. But in the meantime, Colorado has gone No Law and it's impacting everybody else, and the feds seem powerless to stop it. So instead, what they've done is basically encircle this wild west area with barbed wire, and they're trying to control who can go in and who can go out. But they're not letting – I mean – they're embargoing them and putting trade limitations on Colorado, and it's killing a lot of good businesses in Nebraska.

I mean, no oil, for example, or gasoline can get in, and now people in there are fermenting alcohol. They're using crops to make ethanol and they're converting all their cars and machines to ethanol, and they're using more solar and wind power, and they're just becoming completely self-sufficient, and it's killing good Nebraska businesses here that used to do business with people in Colorado. I mean, food, fruits, and vegetables and all this stuff that the feds are stopping from coming in. Umm, it's not just killing the businesses that used to sell them that stuff, but these Coloradans are now becoming self-sufficient and even more powerful. So the whole thing is backfiring. We've got to get – marshal our resources. Instead of fighting wars overseas, we've got to be fighting what I feel like are basically becoming these independent countries inside our own country.

You know, there are people that are still able to come and go out of Colorado. I totally understand why people are trying to get out of there. But I don't understand – it seems like lately there's a greater number of people that are trying to get in. Don't they understand what they're signing up for? It's the wild west there and, look, this country is founded on laws – it's not founded on no law. Thank you very much.

Host: Thank you, Ramona. Bonny is from Chicago, Illinois. Go ahead please, Bonny.

Caller: Good morning, Jason. The thing I'd like to bring up, um, I think the federal government is completely overextended. Um, you know, I just worry about where this country's headed. We have little clue, it seems to me, like about who really launched this atomic annihilation of D.C., New York City, and L.A. Tons of theories, but everybody's suspicious of them and –

Host: Are you with us, Bonny?

Caller: Yeah, I didn't know if you could hear me. Um, all the answers, fingers, seem to point, you know, to one of these fundamentalist groups in the Middle East. But no one knows for sure. And now sprouting up in the midst of our own country are basically areas where the feds have said, "Look – we can't stop people from breaking the law of the land." These No Law people say America, uh, it's founded on freedom to the extent that anybody can do whatever they want, and I disagree with that. I mean, there's already enough murders and it's only going to get worse if there's no law at all. So we've got to do something. Thank you for, uh, listening to my call.

Host: Thank you. Next caller, go ahead, please. Preston from Fredericktown, Ohio. You are on the air.

Caller: Well, yeah, hi. Uh, you know, where I'm concerned is – I'm in – where I live, in the middle of Ohio, there's a lot of Amish here, and what we've seen is the No Law territories movement is expanding, and where the Amish are stepping into this – like this crazy offshoot Amish sect – that doesn't seem to have support from the normal peaceful Amish that we're used to. But the Amish that we're used to are so pacifistic that they're not doing anything to control these people. They're like militant Amish, I guess is the best way to describe them, so their technology is pretty limited, but they do use guns. I've seen them carrying guns. Um, but they don't use vehicles, they don't use electricity. Everything they use is mechanical or with animals, you know, so guns are mechanical, so they'll use guns. They won't use anything digital. They want to be able to take it apart and figure it all out.

But anyways, these Amish are stepping into this power vacuum. Uh, the lack of law enforcement is making this a free-for-all. And we've got parts of Ohio now that you can't drive a car into without being stopped by Amish men on horseback – having your electronics and stuff seized and destroyed by these militant Amish. They're out of control. Uh, they're being, uh you know, they follow a very fundamentalist view of their religion and the world. They're as bad, I believe, as the fundamentalist Islamists that we're trying to fight overseas and that are trying to get over here. I mean, we're saying we don't want the radical Islamists to get over here 'cause we're scared of what would happen. But I mean, we've got radical militant Amish in parts of Ohio. This seems to be very underreported, if at all. And I'm telling you, it's a dangerous thing. These people are starting to go on war parties, I guess you could call them, where they're raiding communities. They're forcing people to change the way they live to be more Amish, to comply with a lot of Amish rules. And I think, um, it's just another dangerous sign of where this country is headed. Thanks.

Host: OK, caller, thank you. I'm not sure what exactly you're talking about. I'm in Ohio, in Cleveland, and haven't seen or heard of any of this. You're rambling a bit there.

Caller: It's not in the cities, but it's all around here. Down here in Knox County anyways; it's out of control with the Amish.

Host: OK. Thank you. Melvin in Burney, California, hello.

Caller: Hi. Thank you, Jason, and thank you for C-SPAN. And I have two thoughts. The first is terrorism is a tactic, not an enemy. Fighting terrorism is like saying we're fighting tanks. It's stupid. We need to know what enemy we're fighting and understand what their motivations are. The second is about No Law. Look, it all started with pot legalization in Colorado,

Oregon, and Washington. I've been thinking a lot about this. Does one person need law? No. Law is only needed if there is more than one person. Is law needed between two people? No, they can keep their distance, and there's no third party to appeal to. Is law needed between mother and child? Father and son? Brother and sister? No – the family can sort things out on their own. Laws are only needed to prop up the powerful and the weak.

How can five hundred thirty-five grey-haired old people, hundreds of miles away, decide how we live our lives – how we work, play, live, and die? I want to talk about, let me just say, that I'm seventy-five years old. I'm watching politics all these years. As these parties have become more polarized, I notice divided government does not work. The government people have made a grave mistake, and now they're reaping the actions against them and appropriately because there's enough of us out here that don't really like the national government. Independence for the states would solve the problem with the two-party system. They wouldn't be the dominant parties because we're so sick of all this garbage. Thank you, that's it.

Host: OK. We have time for one more call. Patty from Idaho is waiting, and Patty, you are a No Law supporter?

Caller: Yes, I am. I'm in Idaho, and I do think this whole country is going to be free and the federal government is going to disappear. I do think we're getting too socialist. Everyone in government who sucks off the back of working men and women, all the parasites in the big cities, all these computer people who make online porn instead of real things and food and shelter, they are going to be at the bottom of the food chain instead of the top.

Host: OK. This will be a big topic for the next few months until voting day in Idaho with a No Law initiative on the ballot. That will do it for the call-in program today on *Feronia Journal*. We'll be right back here tomorrow morning at seven a.m. Eastern, four a.m. Pacific. Have a great day.

TWENTY THREE
cabinet meeting

<u>Minutes of Presidential Meeting in the Feronia Cabinet Room</u>

<u>Topic:</u> Colorado reconnaissance: findings and next steps

At 8:45 a.m. CIA Director Jack Killington informed the president of surveillance photographs showing Colorado citizens occupying federal military bases and weapons sites. President Scott immediately scheduled a meeting of his principal advisers for 9:30 a.m.

<u>Present at the meeting:</u>
President Peter Scott
Tim O'Brien, Secretary of Defense
Francis Pascal, Secretary of State
Jack Killington, Director of the Central Intelligence Agency
General Hunter Warren, Chairman of the Joint Chiefs of Staff
Isabella Matthew, Secretary of Homeland Security
Robert Fitzgerald, Attorney General
Victoria Garen, Colorado Governor in exile
(Vice President Hugh Dryden was scheduled to attend but did not.)

MEETING COMMENCED AT 9:33 AM.

[Muffled laughter and conversations]

President: Isabella?

Secretary of Homeland Security Matthew: Yes, Mr. President, this is a serious development. We hadn't believed the people in Colorado – the No Law rebels – would carry it this far. They'd been denying they were going to build any military of their own. I think we have to eliminate these bases. We can't sit still. The question becomes whether we do it with a sudden, unannounced strike of some sort, or whether we build up the crisis to the point where the rebels take action against us first, and then we can retaliate.

Secretary of State Pascal: The thing for all of us to be very conscious of is there's no such thing as unilateral action by the United States. Any action we take will greatly increase our risks involving other states, our foreign alliances, and forces in other parts of the world, especially our ongoing confrontations in the Middle East.

Secretary of Homeland Security Matthew: I suggest we think very hard about two major courses of action. One is the quick strike. In other words, we make it clear that we're eliminating particular bases, any former American military base or National Guard site that they're occupying. We're not moved to general war; we're simply doing what we said we'd do if Coloradans took this action. Or we're going to decide that now is the time to solve the No Law problem by eliminating all the rebels in Colorado, and Oregon, and maybe even Idaho and elsewhere.

I propose a combination of things to consider. First, we stimulate Congress immediately for prompt action to make it clear that the entire country considers No Law military bases and weapon sites to be a national security threat. Congress could insist that a federal inspection team be permitted to go and look at these Colorado sites to provide assurances they aren't a threat. The No Law leadership will undoubtedly turn that down, but it will be another step in building a political position to support a future invasion by the federal government.

Governor Garen: I think we ought to consider getting some word to Richard Johnson, the president of the No Law Republic of Colorado; Errol Morris, the president of the No Law Republic of Oregon; and Clara Ahlberg – she'll be president of Idaho if the initiative passes there in November. And also Declan Kikas. As the de facto leader of the No Law movement, he may be calling the shots on this. Maybe we can get them to back down.

Secretary of State Pascal: We don't have direct contact with any of them, but perhaps we could make contact through the Colorado ambassador to Cuba or through Oregon's non-voting representative at the United Nations. I think the Coloradan ambassador would be the best channel to try. Communicate privately and tell them we're preparing to take action if they persist in building military capability.

President: What do we need to do in the next twenty-four hours?

Secretary of Defense O'Brien: Sir, we need to do two things: First, we need to develop a specific strike plan. The second thing we have to do is consider the consequences. I don't know what kind of a world we'll live in after we've struck Colorado. How do we stop at that point? I don't know the answer to this.

President: The chances of it becoming a full-on civil war are increased as you step up the talk about the danger to the United States.

Secretary of Defense O'Brien: There are a large number of federal military bases within the No Law territories. The big federal ones in Colorado include the Pueblo Chemical Depot, Fort Carson, Cheyenne Mountain Air Base, and Peterson Air Force Base. Federal troops evacuated these when No Law took over, but there are still a lot of weapon systems, attack aircraft, and military vehicles in place at all of them. It's also worth noting that just sixteen miles north of the Colorado border is the Warren Air Force Base in Wyoming, where we have hundreds of nuclear missiles.

President: Jesus H. Christ.

Secretary of Defense O'Brien: You maybe saw *The Feronia Messenger* story yesterday? No Law officials said they view our checkpoints in and out of Colorado and Oregon as an attack on their sovereign nations. But we need to make it clear that any kind of military capability in any No Law territory is not acceptable. And I think there are certain military actions that we might want to take straightaway. First, to call up highly selective units, no more than one hundred thousand troops. At the time we announce this – and I think that's sometime this week – we can also announce we're openly conducting satellite, airplane, and drone surveillance of Colorado and Oregon, and that we will enforce our right to do so. We make a public statement that we reject any No Law military capability. We also start to tactically position our forces in surrounding states – Wyoming, Nebraska, Kansas, Oklahoma, Texas, New Mexico, Arizona, Utah, and maybe Idaho.

Governor Garen: I suggest no increased federal presence in Idaho – of any kind – until after their No Law vote. We don't want to give Idahoans any more reason to support the movement.

Secretary of State Pascal: I agree.

Secretary of Defense O'Brien: Yep. Noted. We increase our forces in the West – focused on being able to deliver an overwhelming strike anywhere inside Colorado – but take into account the political situation in Idaho.

Secretary of State Pascal: I also think that we need to alert our allies, including consultation with NATO.

Secretary of Defense O'Brien: Mr. President, there are a number of unknowns in this situation that I want to comment on, and I'd like to outline some military alternatives and ask General Warren to expand on them.

But before commenting on either the unknowns or outlining military alternatives, there are two propositions that I suggest we accept as foundations for our further thinking. My first is that if we are to conduct an airstrike against any part of Colorado, we must agree that we will schedule that prior to the No Law military becoming fully operational. I'm not prepared to say when that will be, but I think it's extremely important that our discussion be founded on this premise, because if they become operational before our airstrike, I don't believe we can knock them out before they launch a counterattack – and if Colorado attacks us, there will be chaos throughout the United States.

Uh... secondly, I would submit that any airstrike must be directed not solely against the No Law bases and airfields, but also against civilian airports and key targets inside Colorado cities and towns. We have to send a strong message with overwhelming force. Now, this would be a fairly extensive airstrike, not just a strike against the military sites, and there would be civilian casualties, likely in the low thousands, say five or six thousand. It seems to me these two propositions should underlie our discussion.

Now, what kinds of military action are we capable of carrying out? And what will be the consequences? We could carry out an airstrike within a matter of days. If it were absolutely essential, it could be done within hours. The chiefs would prefer it be deferred for a matter of days, but we're prepared for it to happen quickly. Presumably, political discussions would take place before the airstrike and during. In any event, we'd be prepared, following the airstrike, for an invasion by ground troops. Approximately seven days after the start of the airstrike, a ground-force invasion of Colorado would be possible.

Associated with this airstrike should be some degree of mobilization, implementing a draft. A small mobilization could be carried out with authority granted by Congress. There might be a larger, second phase, and this would require declaring a national emergency. Now, this is very sketchily the military plan. I think you should hear General Warren outline his choice.

General Warren: We're impressed, Mr. President, with the great importance of striking Colorado with all the benefit of surprise. We'll never have perfect timing. What we'd like to do is look at the newest photography, get the layout of the targets, and then take the bastards out without any warning. That does not preclude, I don't think, the political things you've been talking about, but we must do a good job the first time we go in there, pushing one hundred percent as closely as we can. I'm having all the military planners in later this morning, Mr. President, to talk this out with 'em and get their best judgment.

Also among the military actions we should take is significantly tightening our blockade around Colorado to stop more people from going there. So, I'm thinking of three phases: One, an initial pause to plan and prepare so we can do the best job. Then, second, major airstrikes against bases, depots, missile sites, airfields, any sites that we know of. Third, a much stronger blockade. I'd also increase the reconnaissance over Colorado and Oregon.

Then the decision can be made as to whether we invade or not. I think that's the hardest question militarily in the whole business – one that we should look at very closely before we get our feet that deep in the mud in Colorado.

Secretary of Homeland Security Matthew: I agree we should consider attacking only if we can carry it off before these No Law bases and weapons become operational. If we think that Colorado is capable of launching artillery or dropping bombs, frankly, I would strongly urge against the air attack because of the danger to this country if they attack us.

General Warren: We should be fearful, especially of attack aircraft and artillery. We have a serious air-defense problem. I don't know what a No

Law Air Force is capable of, but we must assume that a rebel air force would be capable of penetrating our interior air defenses by coming in low over the mountains and countryside. We should not leave any air force intact and run the risk that they would use that against us. It would be a very heavy price to pay in American lives and give No Law even more power politically.

President: How effective can our takeout be, do you think?

General Warren: It'll never be a hundred percent, Mr. President. We hope to take out a vast majority, but this isn't just one strike, one day, but a continuous air attack for many days, whenever necessary, whenever we discover a target.

President: What's the reason for the Colorado leaders to build military capability? What'd be the reason that they would, uh...

Governor Garen: I'm sure they'd say these are defensive only, to be able to defend themselves if attacked, and they've said they consider the checkpoints around Colorado and Oregon to be attacks on them.

Secretary of Defense O'Brien: I suggest, Mr. President, that if we're involved in several hundred air attacks, it will be very difficult to convince anybody that this isn't a pre-invasion attack. I also think that with this volume of airstrikes, there will be little difference in public reaction between air attacks and a full invasion. So from both standpoints, it seems to me that if you're talking about a general air-attack program, you might as well think about whether we can simply eradicate the whole No Law problem by invading Colorado, then Oregon.

Attorney General Fitzgerald: So, I think there are two alternatives: one, the quick strike; the other, to alert our allies and No Law leaders that there is an utterly serious crisis in the making here. I think we're facing a situation that could lead to war, so we have an obligation to do what has to be done, but do it in a way that gives everybody a chance to back off before it gets too hard. Those are my reactions as of this morning, Mr. President. I naturally need to think about this very hard for the next several hours.

Governor Garen: I don't think we consult too much with other state governors. I think they're fine, but I wouldn't rely on 'em much. The fact is, the country's blood pressure is up, Americans are fearful, and we're getting divided. The President's already said that any time the No Law rebels threaten our security we're going to do whatever must be done to protect ourselves. When you say that, people give unanimous support. I'm not much for pow-wowing with the governors, or Congress, or our allies. We need to act no matter what they say, and we're not going to get much help from them.

CIA Director Killington: At the very least, we probably ought to tell them, though, the night before we attack. There are principal allies and nearby state governors we should communicate with, at least on a twenty-four-hour-notice basis. Certainly ease the surprise a bit.

President: What you're really talking about are two or three different operations. One is the strike on just on the bases. The second is the broader one that Secretary O'Brien was talking about, which is on the civilian airports and on nearby cities. Third is doing both of those things and also at the same time making a much stronger blockade. And then, as I take it, the fourth question is the degree of consultation.

Attorney General Fitzgerald: Mr. President?

President: Yes?

Attorney General Fitzgerald: We have the fifth one, which is the invasion. You're dropping bombs all over Colorado if you do the second, the civilian airports, knocking out their planes, dropping bombs on nearby towns. You're covering much of Colorado. You're going to kill an awful lot of people, and we're going to take an awful lot of heat on it.

President: I think we ought to just take the military bases out and prepare for invasion. An invasion may be where we end up. We're certainly going to do number one; we're going to take out these military bases. The question will be whether we do number two, which would be a general airstrike. Let's prepare for it. The third is the full invasion. At the very least, we're going to do number one, so we ought to be making those preparations.

Secretary of State Pascal: You want to be clear, Mr. President, whether we've definitely decided against a political track. I, myself, think we ought–

President: Let's decide who we talk to and how long ahead.

Secretary of Defense O'Brien: Mr. President, may I suggest that we come back this afternoon prepared to answer three questions. First, should we surface our surveillance? I think this is a very important question at the moment. We ought to try to decide today either yes or no.

President: By "surface our surveillance" …?

Secretary of Defense O'Brien: I mean should we publicly share our satellite imagery showing that the No Law rebels in Colorado are building a military capability? And publicly state that we'll act to take out any offensive weapons? Formally state that we are conducting ongoing surveillance flights with our planes and drones. We'll make the information public.

President: All right.

Secretary of Defense O'Brien: That is one question. A second question is should we precede the military action with political action? If so, on what timing? I think the answer's almost certainly yes. I think particularly of the contacts with Declan Kikas and President Johnson of Colorado. And I think they must be scheduled very carefully in relation to potential military action. There must be a very precise series of contacts with them and indications of what we'll do at certain times following that. And, thirdly, we should be prepared to answer your questions regarding the effect of these strikes and the time required to carry them off.

President: Uh… anything that makes you doubt whether the No Law rebels are really trying to build an offensive capability? How much do we know? I don't mean to question your judgment here, but it will be catastrophic if we attack Colorado on a bad guess. We can't do that.

CIA Director Killington: No. There's no question, sir. It's clear from both the surveillance imagery and reports from people we have on the ground. Colorado is genuinely trying to build its own military capability, repurposing federal bases and weapons. It's clearly an offensive capability. Everyone there already has all the guns they need for self-defense.

[Laughter]

Governor Garen: We need to tune our language for public consumption; we call them "rebels," but they *are* the lawfully elected government in Colorado. They took power with an overwhelming majority in the polls, and they have strong support inside and outside the state. Many Americans don't see them as rebels; they see them as patriots. We need to be sensitive to alienating more citizens and creating even more sympathy for the No Law movement.

Secretary of Defense O'Brien: Mr. President, I suggest we come back early this afternoon to propose a plan and better answer your questions. At two?

President: OK. Thanks, everyone. Let's regroup then.

MEETING ADJOURNED AT 10:02AM

TWENTY FOUR
lists

Be prepared.

           – Scout motto

Thirteen men sat crammed in a family room on wilcox street in chicago, just a few blocks from garfield park. It was a hot and humid august night. Windows were open, letting in the background sounds of sirens and police helicopters. Sitting in one corner of the room was an overflowing, fifty-five-gallon, gray plastic trash can, the visible layers of garbage included cigarette butts, beer and soda cans, fast-food bags and wrappers, and a pizza box. In front of the fireplace was a large wooden television set, the glass screen broken out of it, the electronics removed, and a glass aquarium half-filled with sludgy, green liquid sitting inside it. Some of the men sat on couches, some sat on the crusty, brownish carpet, some stood against the walls.

P-rock, leaning against a wall, said, "And we can get generators and stuff, and power tools and other equipment."

"No. Listen to me," Spit spoke up. He was sitting on a plastic chair that he pushed back on its hind legs when he spoke. "We can't travel across the country with so much stuff. Motorcycles? Pickup trucks? Generators and power equipment? Yeah, we'll need all that, but they're selling that stuff inside colorado. We need to travel light on gear, heavy with cash. Forty of us in the eight minivans, plus two u-hauls max with the basics. We travel light with stuff, heavy with cash; we got to get across the border first. We gotta have two lists."

"Yeah. Smart, Spit," Griffin said. He was standing near the middle of the room. "And listen, we're not takin' any dope with us. Until we leave, we need to sell as much we can to raise funds. But everyone needs to clean up like a baby before we go. No dope's comin' with us."

"Where do we go in?" Ex asked.

"Wood and I keep talking about this," Griffin said. "They got checkpoints on every highway comin' into colorado. No one from outside is allowed in unless you've got special permission, and we don't. So, we can try to sneak in on some rural back road – there's tons of 'em – and we might find a place to cut through where they ain't watchin'. But the feds got cameras and drones on the unmanned perimeter and we don't know the country well enough, so we'd be bumbling around, lookin' for a place to cut in, and they'll spot us and get us. Out there, away from everything, they can shoot us up and make up any story to justify blowin' us away."

Mini said, "Ok. Plan a sounds like *no way*. What's plan b?"

Wood, sitting crammed with others on a brown couch, looked around at each of the men while he spoke. "We go in through one of the big interstate checkpoints and we live-stream it so the whole world can see. We declare ourselves to be political refugees seeking asylum in No Law from a federal government who oppresses us. We make it a political statement. If they're gonna stop us, they'll have to do it by force, in front of the whole world. We live-stream the whole thing off our phones. We never stop moving, the vehicles roll, and we have our guns out and all the woman and the children in full view. We drive through peacefully if they let us, and we drive through shootin' and killin' 'em if they don't. I've got some other ideas, but that's the plan right now."

"Hell yeah!" Mini said, taking his hands out his pockets, waving his fists. "I love it."

Wood said, "It's sixteen hours of driving. We won't do it all in a day. We'll take two days, get close to the border, then stage up close to the entry point and do some recon, plannin', and rehearsals. Then we pick an early morning to go in."

"We should have a *bomb*," Club said. "Somethin' we tell 'em if we press the red button, everyone within five hundred yards of the checkpoint is tomato soup."

"Yeah, bro!" Fish said.

"Except we'd blow ourselves up too, you idiot," Truck laughed.

122

Griffin said, "Guns. We need a lot of guns and ammo. Handguns and assault rifles. Stag a-r fifteens, one for everyone, and nine-millimeter handguns, sig sauers with the twenty-round magazines. We also get a bunch of bulletproof vests, level twos like the pigs use, and some g-h level threes for the guys in front seats, and some five-five-six millimeter green-tip armor-penetrating rounds."

"Pepper hates guns, Griff," Columbus said.

"She's gonna have to get over it, Columbus. Everyone's gonna pack heat. Write all this down, P. For after we get in. We need first-aid kits. Food and water, gasoline, motor oil, seeds, and fertilizer. I read the ground can grow wheat and potatoes good. Every family needs tents, camp stoves, sleeping bags, blankets, water jugs. We need all kinds of tools and equipment for buildin' and farmin'. Make a list of all that and include generators, tools, ropes, extension cords. And remember – no drugs or booze – no crack, no pot, no liquor, no beer. We're done losin' our minds, we're gonna need 'em to survive."

Couch jumped in, "That's a problem, Griff. I need my wine. Jocelyn needs her joints – it's how she calms down. It's how I get through the day. It's all I got to look forward to."

"Then you're not invited, Couch. Leave now. None of that stuff is comin' with us. None of that stuff is goin' 'cause we're gonna be workin' hard, we're gonna be educatin' our kids, and we need every bit of brain cells and time we got to have any chance to figure this all out."

Couch backed off, "Well, at least make sure we got a lot of that lemonade drink mix. We need books, too – a set of encyclopedias and a bible. And some games – cards and chess and checkers. I mean, I hate workin', Griff. I need somethin' to do I enjoy 'cause I *hate* work."

Griffin laughed, "Sure, ok, write it down, P. And money. Everybody who hasn't paid up – and that's most of you – needs to come on and get me their money. Five thousand per person. That goes into the community pot; that's two hundred grand. Then everyone needs another five grand per person for their own expenses, so they're not moochin'. That's enough to buy land with some leftover for whatever we need for at least the first year."

"Where we gonna live, Griff?" Cig asked.

"There's good deals on real estate since no one can get in there, but we're still gonna need a lot of money to buy property. Once we find it, we'll live in tents while we build a big buildin' to start, then off that we can build separate attached areas for the families to have their own rooms. The big buildin' will be a common area, a kitchen and eating area, a gatherin' place we can use for a school and for meetin's. Oh, and once we get land, we're gonna get animals – chickens and pigs will be easy to start with."

P laughed while he spoke, "Animals? Man, we're gonna be *farmin'!* This is gonna be great. We're gonna be in charge. It's crazy, but it makes sense. It's stupid, but it's the smartest thing I've ever done."

"You're right, P," Griffin said. He smiled and looked around the room at his friends. "This time next month, we're finally gonna be free men."

"Or dead," someone laughed.

"We're free either way," Griffin said.

TWENTY FIVE
insanity

People are crazy and times are strange
I'm locked in tight, I'm out of range
I used to care, but things have changed
— Bob Dylan, *Things Have Changed*

I'm losing it, Mark Halberstam thought. *I'm unbalanced.* He sat at his desk and felt his mind begin to wander. The screens in front of him blurred together. His eyes drifted away from the screens across stacks of printouts scattered across his desk: financial statements and legal agreements that all required his immediate attention.

He closed his eyes, and he heard music, drops of sound that formed a melody, and a young woman's voice sang, softly at first then came on stronger. He knew he was imagining the music, but he kept his eyes closed because the hallucination felt good. It was freeing; it let him forget the reality that he could never make everyone happy, that everyone around him was at best slightly disappointed in him, that many hated him or thought he was a fool, that he hated himself.

Pure insanity was the complete lack of logical thought. Sanity was unemotional, calculating, algebraic, and linear. Insanity was hallucinations and irrational conclusions, often based on imagination, emotion, and false perception. To be truly insane would be to lose the ability to tell the difference between sane and insane – a line he hadn't crossed yet, thank god.

But there was an in-between place that he enjoyed visiting more and more often. He could close his eyes and imagine wrapping himself in a fleece blanket, and in a few moments he was standing on the edge of a cliff, looking out into a starry night and down into a black abyss, picking one foot up off the ground and sticking it into the air. The stars glowed in the darkness until several specks of light became a string, then a glowing strand, and then suddenly a whoosh of sound came from the strand towards him and let him forget for a while about his employees who hated him, and his customers who didn't respect him, and Sheila who was using him while he was using her, and his innocent family whom he'd murdered.

With one foot still in the air, he raised both arms, now standing on the edge of the cliff balanced on one foot, a slight, warm breeze holding him up. He was Jesus Christ, arms extended outward, head hung down, all the sins of everyone placed upon him, suffocating him, but there was joy inside him at finally being tortured, finally being blamed for everything, finally accepting all the guilt there ever was. In that moment, he finally felt free. He knew there was no guilt left anywhere else in all of creation – he was carrying all of it. It was suffocating him and it would kill him, but he could finally stop worrying if he was to blame because it was clear that everything was his fault. The uncertainty was over.

Where was the truth hidden? He'd been looking for it for so long, inside himself, outside himself, in religion, science, books, women, money, drugs, travelling, friendship, family, love, hate, sex, chastity, sin, virtue, vice, teachers, education, ignorance, imagination. He could not find the answer, and he could not let the question go, no matter how hard he tried to numb his mind with booze, sex, sports, gambling, and work. Every day brought him closer to the end of his life, and every day he felt further away from any understanding of why he was alive.

He breathed in. He breathed out. Was this life just a meandering dream? He looked at his reflection on the varnished desk. Was truth hidden somewhere it could be found?

Breathe in, breathe out. He looked closer at his reflection, unable to read his own eyes. For a moment, he felt he was looking at a total stranger – what was that man thinking? Why was he here? Then he remembered he was looking at himself, and he looked away.

He heard a keyboard work its way through a melody, one note at a time, a bass beat underneath it, giving the notes a place to rest and connect. He heard a young woman's voice. She sang, "If you want me to stay, I need you to know, I can never let you go." He remembered Sheila had told him that once and it frightened him. He'd wanted to tell her then that he was just using her and lying to her, that he had done whatever it took to have her, but that he would never love her, and that he would eventually abandon her with a ruthlessness that would leave her permanently damaged.

This is all my imagination, he reminded himself. *There's no music. There's no woman singing to me.*

The problem with insanity was that it led to isolation and poverty. The problem with sanity was that it led to absolute boredom – a life sentence worse than death. He had to decide which he preferred, or he had to see if there was a way to balance the two opposites, stir some insanity into the midst of sanity so that there were swirls of color and intensity within his repetitive life of sleep, eat, and work. He had to mix things up while keeping the lid on the blender. That's what he'd been trying to do by cheating on Gaia with Sheila.

What is sanity? he wondered. *Define it. Show it to me.*

He thought of a line from a song he'd heard, "All the truth in the world adds up to one big lie."

There were no answers. There were no absolutes he believed in. There was nothing shown to him that he could be certain wasn't a mirage. *But I have to keep looking; I really have no other choice. I have to do the best I can and see what happens.*

He looked at his calendar and his messages, hundreds of unread emails. Those were real. The day was packed with meeting conflicts and more commitments than two of him could fulfill. *I need to get to work,* he realized. *Stop living in la la land and start making a living. Get back to reality.*

He sighed, clicked on an email, and turned his mind away from searching for truth, focusing instead on drafting the terms of a merger agreement that the lawyers needed two days ago.

TWENTY SIX
foreign policy

No nation can preserve its freedom in the midst of continual warfare.
— James Madison

Excerpts from the textbook *Origin, Evolution, and Current Principles of the American No Law Movement, Fourth Edition,* by Sean McClusky.

America's Global Meddling
In his farewell address to the country, George Washington, the first president of the United States, said, "It is our true policy to steer clear of permanent alliances with any portion of the foreign world."

The inaugural pledge of the third president, Thomas Jefferson, was no less clear: "Peace, commerce, and honest friendship with all nations, entangling alliances with none."

After the Revolutionary War, non-interventionism was America's foreign policy for its first one hundred years, a stance that contrasted with the constant warring of the European nations. From the eighteenth century until the Second World War, the United States was reluctant to enter into foreign conflicts or alliances. In 1823, President James Monroe articulated the non-interventionist Monroe Doctrine: "In the wars of the European powers, we have never taken part, nor does it comport with our policy to do so."

After the Second World War, however, in a dramatic reversal of the founders' intent, the United States pursued alliances with nations across the globe. By the early twenty-first century, hundreds of American bases and hundreds of thousands of U.S. troops encircled the planet. America occupied the world.

The United States had the world's largest military and interfered everywhere. At its peak, America had over eight hundred foreign bases, with soldiers stationed in almost two hundred countries. The United States had more bases in foreign lands than any other empire in history, costing taxpayers almost a trillion dollars per year, with more military spending than the next seven countries combined (see figure 2a). This constant foreign interference resulted in frequent retaliatory attacks on Americans.

figure 2a: United States military spending in the twenty-first century

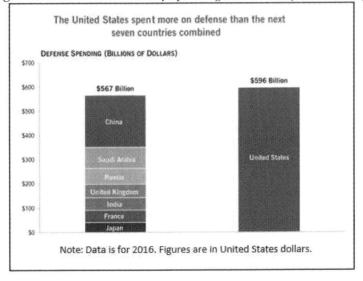

Before the No Law movement, Americans assumed foreign bases were essential to national security and global peace. On the other hand, the idea of foreign bases on U.S. soil was unthinkable; there were zero foreign bases in the United States. While politicians and the mainstream corporate media implied that foreign bases made America safer, No Law leadership argued the opposite, pointing out the numerous ways in which America's foreign meddling made the country less secure and less free.

The Cost of Occupying the World
No Law leaders presented many reasons to question overseas bases. One obvious reason was economic. Overseas bases were expensive. Maintaining installations and troops overseas cost more than the budget of every other government agency.

While foreign bases were costly for taxpayers, they were extremely profitable for the large corporations that influenced U.S. foreign policy with donations to politicians. Corporations such as DynCorp International and Halliburton reaped billions of dollars in business from international bases and twenty-first century wars. American foreign bases brought huge profits to large companies.

No Law leaders complained that spending trillions of taxpayer dollars on overseas bases meant there was less to spend locally on education, transportation, housing, the arts, and healthcare. No Law proclaimed that money spent on foreign bases should instead be spent at home.

Blowback

The No Law movement argued that America's global bases resulted in 'blowback' – unintended, harmful consequences. Foreign bases enabled the launching of military interventions and unconstitutional wars of aggression that resulted in repeated disasters, costing trillions of dollars, millions of lives, and untold decades of destruction from Korea to Iraq.

No Law leaders highlighted how bases abroad led to more war instead of deterring it, made conflict more likely, and created anti-Americanism. For example, the presence of U.S. bases near Muslim holy sites in Saudi Arabia was a major recruiting tool for terrorists such as al-Qaeda and was Osama bin Laden's primary motivation for attacking America, including the World Trade Center and Pentagon attacks in 2001. Ironically, it was America that established, trained, and armed Osama Bin Laden and his al-Qaeda organization to fight the Russians in Afghanistan.

Later, America's subsequent invasion of Iraq shook up an already unstable Middle East and resulted in the establishment of the Islamic State and other fundamentalist Islamic groups that seized power in Iraq, Syria, Libya, and Egypt. These terrorist groups then used captured American weapons and equipment to attack America and her allies.

Rather than stabilizing threatening regions, foreign bases heightened military tensions and discouraged diplomatic solutions. Placing U.S. bases near China, Russia, and Iran, for example, encouraged them to boost their own military spending and activity. No Law leaders asked Americans to imagine how they would respond if China built a base in Mexico, Canada, or the Caribbean. Notably, the most precarious moment during the Cold War – the Cuban missile crisis – was sparked by the construction of Soviet military facilities in Cuba, roughly ninety miles from the U.S. border.

Relying on foreign bases to protect against potential future threats became a self-fulfilling prophecy. Foreign bases ratcheted up tensions and increased military confrontations. U.S. bases turned host countries into targets for foreign powers and terrorists. The foreign bases created the very threats they were supposed to protect against. Far from making the world a safer place, U.S. bases made war more likely.

Federal Surveillance and the Trampling of Liberty

As America's foreign meddling increased, so did retaliatory terrorist attacks inside the country. To battle this domestic terrorism, the federal government increasingly infringed on constitutional liberties with warrantless searches, intrusive surveillance, and by hindering freedom of movement.

Federal trampling of individual rights accelerated after the passage of the USA PATRIOT Act that President George W. Bush signed into law. The ten-letter acronym stood for "Uniting and Strengthening America by Providing Appropriate Tools Required to Intercept and Obstruct Terrorism." The PATRIOT Act allowed for roving wiretaps, warrantless searches of library and business records, and government surveillance of individuals even if they were not linked to any terrorist group.

Opponents of the PATRIOT Act criticized its authorization of indefinite detentions without trial, the permission given to law enforcement to search a home or business without the owner's knowledge, allowing government searches of telephone, e-mail, and financial records without a warrant, and the expanded government access to private library and financial records. Figure 2b compares constitutional protections versus the PATRIOT Act.

The U.S. government engaged in massive unconstitutional surveillance. Secret government documents, published by a variety of whistleblowers, confirmed that the government obtained copies of everything carried on domestic data networks. The government mass-collected the e-mail, web browsing, and phone data of all U.S. citizens under the guise of the PATRIOT Act, without a probable cause warrant. *The New York Messenger* observed, "This isn't a wiretap; it's a country-tap."

After the terrorist nuclear attacks on New York City, Los Angeles, and the District of Columbia, the U.S. Congress passed the Domestic Security Enhancement Act (DSEA). This legislation was dubbed "PATRIOT II" or "Son of PATRIOT" by No Law and other freedom-fighting organizations, such as the American Civil Liberties Union.

figure 2b: Constitutional protections versus the Patriot Act.

The United States Constitution versus The USA PATRIOT Act	
The United States Constitution (Bill of Rights)	The USA PATRIOT Act
Freedom from unreasonable searches:	
Amendment IV: The right of the people to be secure in their persons, houses, papers, and effects, against unreasonable searches and seizures, shall not be violated, and no warrants shall issue, but upon probable cause	The United States government may search and seize Americans' papers and effects without probable cause.
Right to a speedy and public trial:	
Amendment VI: In all criminal prosecutions, the accused shall enjoy the right to a speedy and public trial	The United States government may jail Americans indefinitely without a trial.
Freedom of association:	
Amendment I: Congress shall make no law respecting an establishment of religion, or prohibiting the free exercise thereof; or abridging the freedom of speech, or of the press; or the right of the people peaceably to assemble	To assist terror investigations, the United States government may monitor religious and political institutions without suspecting criminal activity.
Right to legal representation:	
Amendment VI: In all criminal prosecutions, the accused shall... have the assistance of counsel for his defense.	The United States government may monitor private and privileged conversations between attorneys and clients and deny lawyers to Americans accused of crimes.
Freedom of speech:	
Amendment I: Congress shall make no law ... abridging the freedom of speech ...	The United States government may prosecute librarians or keepers of any other records if they tell anyone the government subpoenaed information.
Right to liberty:	
Amendment VI: In all criminal prosecutions, the accused shall enjoy the right to a speedy and public trial... and to be informed of the nature and cause of the accusation... and to have the assistance of counsel for his defense.	Americans may be jailed without being charged or being able to confront witnesses against them. U.S. citizens (labeled "unlawful combatants") have been held incommunicado and refused attorneys.

The DSEA expanded the powers of the federal government, including:
- Creation of a DNA database of Americans
- Criminalization of encryption to conceal communications
- Expansion of the list of crimes eligible for the death penalty
- Removal of prohibitions against federal agencies spying on citizens
- Authorized the Federal Bureau of Investigation to conduct searches and surveillance without warrants
- "Tattle-tale protection" – Exemption from liability for people who turned someone's private information over to the government
- Prohibition of public disclosure of citizens arrested by the government
- Automatic denial of bail for persons accused of federal crimes, reversing the burden-of-proof principle

The DSEA legislation was signed into law despite strong protests from a number of groups, including No Law, the Electronic Frontier Foundation, the American Civil Liberties Union, the Library Freedom Project, and the Bill of Rights Defense Committee.

figure 2c: Twenty-first century political cartoon by Richard Bartholomew

No Law Remonstrance

In his farewell address, President Dwight D. Eisenhower famously warned about the insidious effects of what he dubbed "the military-industrial complex," the vast national security state. He said, "We must guard against the acquisition of unwarranted influence by the military-industrial complex. The potential for the disastrous rise of misplaced power will persist."

But despite Eisenhower's grave warning, Americans assumed that foreign meddling and overseas bases made them safer. Before No Law, support for America's imperialist strategy had remained the consensus among politicians, national security experts, military officials, journalists, and almost everyone in Feronia's power structure. Opposition to maintaining overseas bases and troops was pilloried as peacenik idealism.

No Law leadership successfully convinced a growing number of followers that in reality, America's meddling foreign policy was too expensive, and it didn't make America safer; rather it made America – and everyone else on the planet – less secure and less free, damaging lives at home and abroad.

TWENTY SEVEN
interview

Corby Myers felt nervous. He scrutinized the two tall, silent, young men armed with black machine guns. He looked over at his assistant, Molly, then at his producer, Luke; they seemed calm, which helped him keep it together. He glanced down, checking his reflection in the polished wood table. He looked at the shelves sitting against the rustic cabin walls, overflowing with books: science, philosophy, Tolkien. An anonymous man sat on the other side of the room, reading. The man hadn't spoken, he just sat there, silently.

Corby's body tensed as he heard a vehicle approach, metal doors slam, and then voices from outside. The cabin door opened, and three men entered, also carrying machine guns. Then Declan Kikas himself entered, wearing tan work pants, hiking boots, and a red and tan flannel shirt over a white t-shirt. His thick gray hair ran somewhat wild on the edges and his long, sturdy stride appeared to bind his arms to his sides. He had a small, relaxed smile on his face. Kikas appeared unarmed, but two more men with guns followed him. *Seven men with machine guns in here,* Corby thought. *And I still have no clue who the man in the corner is.*

The new men with guns seemed tense, ready to blow Corby away at the slightest provocation, yet Kikas himself – a hunted fugitive – seemed calm and fully in control. Corby smiled and stood up to say hello, but his smile got stuck, frozen for too long. Everyone was looking at him. *What's wrong with me?* Corby thought. *Get it together!*

After an eternal moment, Corby found control of his frozen nerves. "Hi, Declan. We've never been introduced, but I'm – I'm Corby Myers."

"I know who you are. You're famous," Declan said.

"Hey, I could say the same about you," Corby laughed. "I want to thank you for seeing me and being on *Indicium*. This interview is going to be seen all over america and the world. People are fascinated with your message, with the No Law philosophy, and by the conflicts between that philosophy and the federal government. You don't mind if I call you an anarchist, do you?"

Declan shrugged. "Technically, a revolutionary."

"Whatever. The episode we did on the No Law movement was one of our most popular ones. Luke – my producer – and I, we've wanted to interview you for a long time. And that time has definitely come."

"Maybe."

"I feel it's apparent, to anyone who's hip to what's going on, that our government has thrown the constitution straight out the window. You and your followers are being painted as evil terrorists. I am *not* one of those people. *Today,* they hunt *you* down because you preach No Law; *tomorrow,* they come after *me* because they feel what *I* say is threatening. Where does it all end? That's my angle."

Kikas sat down quietly, looking at the wood table. Corby sat down across from Kikas, looked at Luke, and then back at Kikas. "My problem, Declan, is you don't exactly inspire empathy. I need your help. I have an interview with senator Wayne Gayle, and I'm telling ya, Declan – he makes you look real bad. I have an interview with the federal prosecutor and the government's psychologist. *They* paint you as the evilest man alive. What we need now is *you.* You haven't talked to the press since your escape. Now, two months before the huge idaho vote, you give an exclusive interview and the whole world will see it. This is a media event. The network is running promos everywhere! It's on prime time! Everyone will watch it. *Television history,* my friend. The first sit-down, in-depth interview with the world's most charismatic fugitive, the most dangerous political rebel ever, while he's on the run for his life!"

"Sounds good."

"Everyone is gonna be looking at you, Declan, listening to your words. Sell 'em on your sanity. You're composed, you're articulate; you're obviously not a nut. We'll shame 'em into dropping the whole thing. Whattaya say?"

Declan said softly, "I say, let's go for it."

::<>::<>::<>::<>::<>::<>::<>::<>::<>::

INSERT - TELEVISION FILM - "INDICIUM"

TV ANNOUNCER: Right after the game, stay tuned for a special episode of *Indicium*. Declan Kikas is the *most dangerous man in america*, but Corby Myers isn't afraid to meet him *one-on-one*. He'll confront the leader of the national rebellion. Is Kikas *insane?* An *american maniac?* Or is he a terrorist who belongs where our government says – *in the grave?* Be sure to stay tuned for...

LOGO for INDICIUM rolls to loud cue-in.

MUSIC and TV ANNOUNCER: And now, Corby Myers goes head to head with outlaw Declan Kikas. Straight from a secret location, just two short months before Idaho's historic vote to become the *third* No Law republic. Is he a *madman* or a *terrorist? Let america be the judge.*

CORBY MYERS is standing in front of a sign beside a scenic two-lane highway; white letters painted on brown wood say, "WELCOME TO COLORFUL COLORADO".

CORBY MYERS: *No Law.* I'm standing where it began. No Law was born in colorado, a fringe movement led by forgotten misfits. But in sparsely populated counties, it began winning local elections... and it spread. Now, statewide referendums have abolished all federal law in colorado and oregon. Idaho will likely be next. It seems there's no stopping the No Law movement. This rebellion has torn across the west with a vengeance right out of the bible. In less than a year, this beautiful stretch of american landscape has peeled away from the rest of the country and become a candy land of anarchy. This mayhem is the fulfillment of one man's fantasy – the hedonistic daydreams of Declan Kikas. He's a philosopher, farmer, and engineer. Many call him a freedom-crazed narcissist and psychopath. The american government has sentenced him to death and named him the most wanted fugitive in the world. In a first-ever exclusive interview, Declan Kikas meets with *me* at an undisclosed, heavily fortified location.

CUT TO: DECLAN KIKAS (Close-up of face – in a chair, very calm, a pleasant smile)

KIKAS: How ya doin' today?

Across from him is CORBY, with a serious intensity, half-glasses, consulting his yellow legal pad of notes.

CORBY: Declan Kikas. Thank you for this time. I have a few questions I'd like to start with, do you mind?

KIKAS: (Smiles) Let's roll.

CORBY: Declan, what motivated you to become a political leader? You were never active in politics until your fifties when you became a revolutionary. Now, you're america's most wanted man, sentenced to death for treason. *What happened* that changed you?

KIKAS: I got tired of pretending that phoniness is real. The phonies are in control of this society, and everyone has to pretend they're real to survive. Bankers are phonies dealing out phony money. Politicians are phonies. Corporations are phony, so everyone who works for them is phony. And I saw that the only truth is inside us and in nature. Nature is how god speaks to us – through the sun, the stars, the ocean, the animals – those are his words, unfiltered, untranscribed, immune to human bias and fallibility. I listened to nature. I put human words aside and soaked in god's message.

Another thing that impacted me – I remember after one presidential election, people in some parts of the country were furious. There were riots in new york, los angeles, portland. In san francisco, ninety percent of the votes were for the loser, and I was really sympathetic to the protesters. Millions of people didn't want a man to be their leader, and yet a bunch of people they'd never met in ohio had decided who would be in charge of them. I watched these people rioting. I saw states pass drug laws in direct contradiction of federal law, and I saw the future. The united states will dissolve. The federal government won't be overthrown violently; it will just slowly lose power. It will pass laws, like marijuana being illegal, but states will just ignore them.

All I'm doing in leading the No Law movement is opening the door to fate. It will happen without me. I'm simply an usher, showing people to their seats for the show that's going to happen whether I'm there or not.

CORBY: When did you first start rejecting all authority, despising anyone telling you what to do? Hating the government? Valuing individual freedom above all else?

KIKAS: Birth... I was thrown into a flaming pit of tyranny and oppression, forgotten by god. (Laughs)

CORBY: What do you mean by that?

KIKAS: I mean I came from oppression. My dad had control over all of us kids. (Chuckles) You know. *Shut up. Sit down. Don't do that.* It was all my fate.

CORBY: No one is born evil, Declan. It's something you learn. Let's talk about your father. How was he murdered? You were thirteen years old when he died. Is that–

KIKAS: (Mood immediately changes, darkens) I'm not evil. I didn't kill my father and I don't want to talk about that... (He sits quietly for a moment) Please.

CORBY: Ok, ok, Declan. Let's go on to something else. I understand you read the bible.

KIKAS: I read everything.

CORBY: But then your morality is based on a christian view, a morality that not everyone shares.

KIKAS: Every faith shares the same moral principle. Love God. Love yourself. Love others as you love yourself.

CORBY: What about those with no faith?

KIKAS: Everyone has faith in something. Every moral judgment rests on faith, not fact – on belief, not certainty. And faith is personal, different for each person. Combine that with Christ saying that we're all god, that god is inside of us. You realize that absolute holiness is absolute freedom to be yourself. They're the same.

CORBY: Jesus said that god is inside us?

KIKAS: When asked by the pharisees when the kingdom of god would come, Jesus replied, *the kingdom of god is within you.* Fascinating. Christ didn't say it's in heaven, or in the temple, or in the bible, or in the future. (Pointing at CORBY) God is inside *you.* (Pointing at himself) God is inside *me.*

CORBY: But Jesus also said, *render unto Caesar what is Caesar's.* He preached spiritual revolution. Christ didn't preach political revolution like you.

KIKAS: No Law *is* a spiritual revolution – it just appears political because the federal government has crushed man's spirit. Who is Caesar? I insist that Caesar be someone I can meet and talk to, not a stranger propped into power by corporations whose only moral value is profit. I believe government should be local. Man's life belongs to himself and to god.

CORBY: It *almost* sounds logical when you say it.

KIKAS: It's completely logical. That's why the government hates me, just like the pharisees hated Christ. I am the american Jesus Christ. Christ was a jew, and the jewish establishment nailed him alive to a board for saying that the jews didn't have to listen to the pharisees. I'm american, and the american government has sentenced me to death for saying that no one needs to listen to the government.

CORBY: You refer to Christ, but No Law is inconsistent with the teachings of the bible – the bible's values of charity and restraint, versus a No Law philosophy of anything's allowed.

KIKAS: No Law is completely consistent with the bible, with every religion. Virtue only occurs voluntarily, never by force. Take the virtue of charity. Coloradans now give freely to the poor, without being forced by the government. There's more virtue in No Law than in the rest of america.

Every religion emphasizes that life is a struggle. Christ promised, "The poor you will always have with you". Everyone will live the life prophesied by Ecclesiastes, with a time for every season.

CORBY: (Focusing in with indignation) Alright, Declan, enough with the sunday school lessons. Let's get *real*. Why this *purity* you feel about freedom?

KIKAS: You might never understand. You and I, Corby, we're different species. I used to be you, then I evolved. From where I'm standing, you're an ape. I'm still evolving, while you're living in a mirrored cage, only seeing different reflections of yourself. You sell fear for a living. I give people their freedom.

CORBY: Explain that.

KIKAS: (Laughs) Corby, you just gotta sit still long enough. If you truly sit still, you clear your mind, and you open it up to nature, then it will come clear to you like it did to me that first time. That's when I knew my one true calling.

CORBY: And what's that?

KIKAS: I'm a natural born rebel against big government. Peaceful revolution is my purpose. It's what I was born to do. I will topple the united states government or die in my pursuit of that singular goal.

CORBY: How do you feel about the fact that you're never gonna walk free again? You'll always be looking over your shoulder.

KIKAS: (Smiling) Says who?

CORBY: Says the united states government.

KIKAS: (Laughing) When have they ever been right?

CORBY: But is it really worth it? Is tearing apart the country over your idea of freedom worth being on the run? Having a death sentence hanging over your head? Always looking over your shoulder? Worth being separated from your wife and family – maybe for the rest of your life? You haven't held your grandchildren in more than a year. *Is it worth it?*

KIKAS: Is an instant of purity worth a lifetime of lies? Yeah.

CORBY: What's the purity? The freedom to do whatever you want?

KIKAS: Freedom's only part of it. Truth is the other.

CORBY: Freedom to the point of extinction? What if preserving the human race requires limits on freedom – to prevent us from destroying ourselves?

KIKAS: If there's no freedom, then we're already extinct. Without freedom, we're machines. Without freedom, we're not human.

CORBY: What about man's obligation to his fellow man?

KIKAS: No one has any obligation to anyone else, only charity he gives freely. Government is evil when it declares rights that make men slaves. For example, if I have a right to healthcare and you're the only other man alive, then you must provide me healthcare. If I have a right to housing and food and you're the only other man alive, then you must provide for me – you're

141

my slave. Life and liberty are the only rights government should protect. Charity must be voluntary.

CORBY: When they catch you, Declan, you'll be executed. At the very least, you'll spend the rest of your life in prison.

KIKAS: I've got a much bigger problem than prison, or losing my life. I've got my immortal soul to think about. Prison is a temporary inconvenience. I'm talking about things that are permanent.

CORBY: But aren't you afraid of dying? Everyone is.

KIKAS: I'm not scared of death. There was this physicist at the ohio state university, a guy named Johnny Twain. I heard him speak at a conference in boston. This guy was a computer nut, but he was also a quantum physicist. He was talking about how the universe is constructed, and he convinced me that there are multiple universes, multiple realities, and that made me brave. I know there's nothing to be scared of. I don't know what ever happened to that guy. I wish I could meet him again.

CORBY: What did Johnny Twain say that made you fearless?

KIKAS: He pointed out that every historical and future reality is just a distinct arrangement of subatomic particles. After you've thought about that enough, you lose the ability to be afraid.

CORBY: Don't our individual freedoms conflict with each other? *My* freedom to drive ninety miles an hour down an alley jeopardizes *your* freedom to walk safely down that alley. And this is where government comes in, giving us rules that protect us.

KIKAS: Freedom doesn't mean that it's ok for me to hurt someone. If I hurt another person, I'll be held accountable by other free men. They might take my life if they decide that is what justice demands. And speed limits can be done locally, we don't need speed limits in idaho legislated by feronia.

Everything starts with liberty, with freedom. Everything. Freedom to say what you want to say, freedom to do what you want to do. Our two highest values are liberty and truth. Liberty is first – because truth follows freedom. Like Christ, we preach that no one has a monopoly on the truth – no president or king, no pope or imam, no scientist or university, no government. If we hold the values of freedom and truth above all else, then we will all have lives worth living.

CORBY: But what is justice? Who gets to decide what is just?

KIKAS: Or asked more precisely – what is truth? Pontius Pilate asked Jesus Christ this eternal question, *and Christ would not answer him!* Everyone should find that fascinating. Finally, someone gets to ask god what the truth is! We're all asking this same question in our thoughts, dreams, prayers, and actions in every moment of our lives, and god never gives us any clear answer, and when asked directly by Pilate, he said nothing!

Pilate is one of the people I admire most in the bible because he's one of the most uncertain, never sure, always looking for evidence and other perspectives – from his wife, the pharisees, from Herod, and finally from god himself. He makes a sincere inquiry, and god's silence is his answer. Pilate is all of us, pleading for the truth to come from someone else, and it won't.

CORBY: Ok, so no one person knows the truth. Shouldn't we be guided then, by our collective wisdom, through government?

KIKAS: No one person knows the truth for *anyone else*. But each person *does* know the truth for *themselves*. So we must limit making laws that restrict individual freedom. And when we do make them, they must be local.

CORBY: Life is dangerous without government. Doesn't it become a wild west where the strong exploit the weak? Where power wins over justice?

(CORBY sips from can of COCA-COLA)

KIKAS: The strong use the power of the federal government to exploit the weak. And the powerful use federal laws to shield themselves from justice. The statistics show that crime is much lower in the No Law territories than in most of the incarcerated states of america. And why is that? Because anyone tempted to commit a crime in colorado or oregon knows he'll suffer the consequences of justice, instead of being able to hide behind the law.

Remember, No Law nations have laws. There are courts, there is law enforcement, but this is at the *local* level, where people can hold the system accountable and influence it directly, which they can't do at the federal level where corporate lobbyists rule with money. People can personally meet those who pass and enforce the laws. This is how men are supposed to live, self-governing in agreement with their fellow man, not accepting dictates from faceless politicians working for corporations.

CORBY: You're saying it's ok for people to disobey the nation's laws?

KIKAS: Yeah. Many times, being a law-abiding citizen is evil. If you lived in germany in the nineteen-forties it would be virtuous to break the law to save jews. If you lived in america in the eighteen-hundreds, it would be virtuous to break the law to free slaves.

Laws are written by those in power to perpetuate their power. The american government has sanctioned slavery, it's assassinated american citizens with unmanned drones, it's killed tens of thousands of innocent civilians, it's repeatedly launched undeclared wars against people who've never attacked us. All lawful, *and all evil.*

In nazi germany the law required you to turn in jews to be murdered. If you disobeyed the law, you were sentenced to death, like I've been. We've faced the same circumstances in this country with slavery and immoral wars. And now, with these blockades, our nation is turning its military on its own citizens. Ominous times are approaching. The only just course is resistance.

The overarching goal of the federal government is to make us obedient, patriotic, law-abiding citizens. And if it's unable to elicit such strong feelings, then it would have us be neutral, to be content with beer and mindless entertainment.

CORBY: What about the environment? Don't we need national government to protect our shared natural resources?

KIKAS: Only through No Law can both civilization and the natural world survive. For example, a corporation is a legal entity that protects individuals from being held accountable for their actions. Federal law allows corporations to rape nature faster than it can ever recover, with individuals profiting from the rape but with no individual held responsible! The apparatus of the corporation steals, and no person is held accountable for the theft. A corporation acts without any conscience, and this sociopathic structure is protected by federal law! *This* is ruining the environment.

The No Law nations of colorado and oregon obliterated the legal structure of the corporation. Corporations are immoral. How can men act without being held individually accountable for their actions? If I pour poison into the ground and it reaches my neighbor's well, I'm guilty of a crime. But if a corporation does this, then no individual is responsible; in fact, individuals profit from the crime, from dividends and a rising stock price, while bearing no responsibility. No man should escape responsibility for his actions, and in No Law no one does.

CORBY: But without a national government, how do we agree on the rules to live by?

KIKAS: When the constitution was written, the fastest way to communicate was on horseback. It made some sense to elect someone in the community to be a spokesperson, to travel thousands of miles and collaborate on our behalf. But horses have been replaced by the internet. We don't need representatives to travel for us. We can collaborate across geographies ourselves, online. There's no longer a need for national government.

CORBY: Is No Law building a military in colorado?

KIKAS: The federal blockades are acts of war and we will defend ourselves.

CORBY: I'll take that as a yes. Colorado is building a military capability in case of war with the american government.

(View from behind KIKAS's shoulder, CORBY turns head one-eighth, eyes into the camera.)

CORBY: Civil war may be upon us, and we are talking with the mastermind of this american armageddon, Declan Kikas. We still have *much* more to talk about, so *stay tuned*. And later, we'll talk with superstar actress Jennifer Hawn. She's often travelled to Colorado, and you'll get to hear her astonishing perspective on the No Law movement *and* get a sneak preview of her upcoming blockbuster film. We'll be *right back* after these messages.

INSERT - LOGO for INDICIUM rolls - CUE OUT

CUE IN – COCA-COLA advertisement (60 Sec)

INSERT - 120 seconds of ADS before returning to *INDICIUM*

TWENTY EIGHT
west

Mark Halberstam walked along a two-lane country road, passing field after field, houses interspersed, seeing no one. *Maybe I'm a ghost, wandering alone forever*, he thought. It was afternoon; the september sun had moved past its warmest point. He pushed himself forward, one step at a time – west, west, *west*. His direction was simple – *west*. Follow the sun until the end. He'd left every other purpose behind.

I'm finally done living lies. I'm starting over, I'll put one foot in front of the other until I'm in colorado and I'm finally free... free to live or free to die... but free...

He'd left philadelphia last night around two in the morning, only twelve hours earlier, but it seemed like years ago. It was tough to imagine his old life now; it felt like he'd always been walking and that everything else before this long walk had been a dream, a story once told about a different man.

::<>::<>::<>::<>::<>::<>::<>::<>::<>::

Last night, Mark sat in front of the television watching an interview with Declan Kikas, the leader of the No Law terrorists. He'd gotten drunk, downing drink after drink, captivated by every word Kikas said.

Sheila distracted and annoyed him whenever she intermittently appeared. "It smells like a brewery in here," she said at one point. God, the never-ending nagging – how much of it was a man supposed to endure? That was all she seemed to do – nag him and goof around on her stupid phone, playing candy-cane games and posting pictures of herself looking hot doing nothing.

He ignored her comment but opened his next few beers as quietly as possible to keep them off her running tally. After the program, he'd gotten

146

up to get ready for bed and realized he was blotto – everything tilted and he was almost unable to stand. It took effort to fake being upright. Walking through the house, he kept imagining strange glows under the furniture – as if the underside of every couch and dresser was lined with soft, purple light.

"Are you ok?" Sheila had called out to him from the bedroom while he sat in the bathroom with the window open, inhaling as much fresh air as he could. The outside air was like medicine. He could feel it enter his lungs and work its way into his bloodstream, clearing a path through the fog in his mind, pushing away the vomitous, alcoholic ideas and depression inside him. He'd wished he could take Sheila's words and forge them into a spear and stab her with them, or just grab a hammer and beat her. *I'm fine, you stupid nag. Just leave me alone to drink myself to death and quit interfering.*

Instead of killing Sheila, he'd ignored her, started the shower water, and brushed his teeth, skimming the feronia messenger headlines on his phone while waiting for the shower water to get steaming hot.

After showering, he air-dried, read more of the news, then got under the covers beside Sheila. But sleep was impossible. He kept thinking about the television interview with Declan Kikas. His eyes seemed stuck open, staring at the ceiling, and yet he was too physically exhausted to get up and get a sleeping pill. Anyway, he was tired of taking pills. He'd already drunk too much booze. Next to him, Sheila slept soundly.

As he lay in bed, staring at the textured ceiling, he started to see images of Gaia, his dead children, and american indians. They took turns floating above him within the white plaster peaks and valleys. He could see that they were ok. They knew everything he'd done, but they were in a place where they could forgive him. The images spoke to him, telling him that it was time to leave.

The patterns on the ceiling shifted, and his son Ethan came into focus and spoke to him. "Just do it, dad, it's ok. I knew before because I saw your texts. I didn't tell anyone, until we got here and they saw. I was so angry and hurt, but now I've seen almost everything, enough to know that you're fine, that the only sin you can commit is against yourself. No one is ever the victim of anyone else, just themselves, and you must save yourself. You need to go. *Go.* Leave. Leave tonight, dad. You know you must."

"I do know it," Mark said. "But I still don't understand *how* I know it, and most of all I don't understand *why*? I know I have to leave, but I don't understand *why*?"

His own face had appeared above him, frightening and fascinating him. His floating face spoke so loudly that he worried Sheila would wake up. "Life is a game and the game is a maze. There is never failure in a maze; every dead end is necessary. Every dead end is to be celebrated because you're closer to finding the correct route."

The ceiling patterns had swirled, his face faded away, and the textured ceiling became his old family room in his manhattan apartment. He saw a scene he'd forgotten. Just beginning to remember its horribleness made him close his eyes; he felt like he'd been punched in the stomach while a bat was swung into his knees. Standing in the family room was himself and his son, Ethan. It was last april, just a few weeks before the bombs. He was forcing Ethan to stand still, facing the glowing embers in the fireplace.

"Close your eyes. I'm not going to hurt you," Mark said. "Do you believe me?"

"Yes," Ethan answered, eyes closed.

Mark twisted his torso, raised his arm back, and punched Ethan in the stomach as hard as he could, rocking his small frame. Ethan was shocked, bent over gasping, trying to find a way to breathe, and stunned – too stunned to cry.

"I lied," Mark said. "Just stand still. Keep your eyes closed. I'm not going to hurt you again, ok?"

Ethan didn't say anything. He was bent over, his mouth open, still trying to breathe.

"Ok?" he repeated, louder, yelling.

"Ok," Ethan whispered, almost unable to speak.

"Do you believe me?"

"Yes."

Mark lifted his left foot, his soccer foot. He'd scored so many goals with that foot as a soccer star in college. He kicked hard, his instep slamming into Ethan's bottom, and his son was forced to stumble forward several steps, almost falling to the floor, still holding his stomach from the punch.

"I lied," Mark said. "But I'm not going to do that again, ok?"

Ethan didn't answer.

"I'm not going to do that again. Just stand there and I won't hurt you. Do you believe me?"

After a long moment, Ethan said, "Yes."

Wham! He kicked him in the back of the knees and Ethan fell, collapsed onto the ground, sobbing now. And now Mark felt his own tears welling up in shame and total rage.

"I lied," he said. "But I won't do it again, ok? Do you believe me?"

"No."

"Yeah, I don't blame you. And that was just three lies in a few minutes. Imagine what it's like being lied to every day for months. I should have done that to you years ago and maybe we wouldn't have this problem now."

Ethan didn't say anything. He looked off somewhere distant.

"Get in there. Do your trigonometry. Come show me every thirty minutes what you've gotten done."

"Ok." Ethan was shaking, his arms, voice, and legs vibrating involuntarily from the overdose of adrenaline racing through his system. Mark had never hit him before, ever. Now, he was beating him repeatedly like he was an animal.

His mind raced. He hated himself for beating him, but he hated Ethan more for leaving him no choice. If Ethan told anyone, he could go to jail for abuse. *Don't admit anything,* he reminded himself. *Don't say yes or no – just tell them you want to talk to a lawyer before answering any questions.* Did his lawyer know anything about domestic violence law? About child abuse? Was it child abuse? Or was it his responsibility as a father to kick this spoiled, lazy, lying brat in the butt in the hope that maybe, finally, before it was too late, he could get things figured out. Otherwise, life was going to beat Ethan down harder than Mark ever could, and he wouldn't be standing when it was all over. He'd be flat on the ground, working minimum wage, hoping to be promoted to assistant manager at burger king, with three kids and an always-exhausted wife in a two-bedroom basement apartment, with the television always on, the lingering smell of cheap macaroni and cheese and microwaved hot dogs always present.

He didn't beat Ethan just out of rage and frustration; it was truly a last attempt to fix the problem – like electroshocking depressed people or lobotomizing violent ones. He and Gaia had tried everything short of violence – talking, cajoling, ritalin, psychologists, private tutoring, grounding, taking away his trip to hawaii. Every other carrot and stick had been used up; the only thing they hadn't tried was beating him until he shook and cried. He was the only person who could do that; Gaia could never do it – a stranger couldn't. Only a father could. Maybe Ethan would hate him and never forgive him, but he could live with that if it finally got his head straight. It was impossible to ground him because he didn't want to drive or go out; he liked being alone on the couch with the dog and a guitar. He had no real ambition at all. Ethan seemed to enjoy living a life of vague, drowsy, out-of-focus experiences, no responsibilities, and no decisions.

He hated hurting his son, but he hated more to think of him going into the world as he was, with no self-discipline or ability to work hard. He was out of options after this. Beating Ethan was the last thing he could think of, and he wouldn't do it again. After this, he had to sink or swim on his own.

Ethan's face faded and slid away. Mark wanted to cry out for him and tell him to come back because he'd forgotten to tell him that he was sorry, so sorry, so sorry. "I wanted everything to be perfect for you but I'm the one who messed it all up, and for no reason at all, and I'm so sorry."

Then Gaia's face had faded in. He wanted to hide from her, although he knew that was impossible. He wanted to try to explain why he was in bed with Sheila, although Gaia must already know everything now, so there was nothing to explain. She knew the truth, so lies were a complete waste of time.

"Ethan knows you're sorry," Gaia said. "You don't need to say anything. And words don't matter anyway. Only actions do. You know that more than most people, Mark."

"Yes," Mark said, "only actions matter."

"You know that you need to leave. You need to head west to No Law, to colorado."

"Yes. Somehow, I do know that."

"But you don't know why?"

"Right."

"Search yourself, Mark. Search beyond your selfish desires. Search beyond the confines of competition. Search into yourself, into a truth buried deep inside you, that only you know is there, that only you can translate and decipher. Once you find it, you can live it. You can bring your truth to life."

Mark had lain still and stared, then closed his eyes. He saw dim forms behind his closed eyelids, and he saw himself living in a cabin in the mountains. There was a chicken coop, a small spring with fresh water, a rifle mounted on wooden pegs. He saw a fishing pole. There was a bookshelf with the bible, Huckleberry Finn, an illustrated book of Aesop's fables, and a hardbound journal that he wrote in every day, making notes about his garden, the fish he'd caught, the game he'd killed, a diary of his new life.

"Yes. I'm supposed to be free of all this. I'm supposed to be simpler. And only then maybe I can become a good person, and save my immortal soul."

"Yes," Gaia said softly. "Yes, my love. Yes, my dearest."

"I've felt trapped for so long, forever maybe, by my parents, and authority, and by rules that I could never understand. I just simply trusted the rules, even though I never understood them or wanted to live within them. Then I felt trapped by you, by the kids. And I've been trapped by my competitiveness, the need to win, the terror of losing. And most of all I've been trapped by my selfishness, an insatiable addiction to more money, more sex, more pleasure, more, more, more – always more, always more, always more. And every time I tried to be good it was all pretend, it was all acting, the whole time I was just doing it for some reward from someone else, never because it was what I truly wanted to do. And so I was the most broken of all, while all the time thinking that I was the most whole."

"Yes," Gaia said. "Your spirit is diseased; your mind is contaminated. At times, you've tried to become good, but it was always for someone else, which meant it was always for no one. Because the truth, Mark, is that you must love others *as* you love yourself. '*As*' is the key, the word that too many people disregard, and yet it is the most crucial one. Are you listening to me, my love? My darling?"

"Yes, I am, Gaia. Yes. And I just want you to know that I love you so much, and I'm so sorry for anything I've ever done to hurt you."

"Don't be afraid. Don't worry about me. You can only hurt yourself and you've done so. But you can start to heal if you get on the road and go west. Go tonight. Take nothing with you. Take nothing for the journey – no car, no bag, no water, no money, no extra shirt."

"Ok, I'll go."

The textures on the ceiling had closed back into themselves, swirled, come to a stop, and then stillness. He'd gotten up and left, without waking Sheila.

::<>::<>::<>::<>::<>::<>::<>::<>::<>::

And now, here he was, walking west. He'd disobeyed his dream, bringing his phone along. He kept checking it so often that he'd killed the battery by ten in the morning.

He remembered something else Gaia had told him: "I am with you always. You will walk on your way securely, and you will not stumble."

Easy for Gaia to say, safe in her afterlife within the textured ceiling. *I'm out of my mind. I'm out here on the road with no plan, no money, no license, no nothing, all because I had some stupid crazy dream about Gaia and Ethan and native americans speaking to me from the textured ceiling. It wasn't real – it was a dream. I need to just stop, go home, stop being crazy.* But he knew that going back home to his billions and his supermodel girlfriend was even more insane than walking forward with nothing. Going west – broke, alone, and hopeless – was the sanest thing he could do.

I just wish I had some kind of companion, he thought. He remembered the poodle, Mister Whiskers, and felt guilt for killing the dog the same way he'd killed his family, realizing this was the first time he'd even thought of the animal since new york city was nuked. *I can't be scared. Native americans travelled alone with nothing, and they lived off the land. But the land has changed,* he thought. There's no wildlife anymore, there's no wild fruits and vegetables, there's just paved roads, private property, and fences. Helping a strange man wasn't on anyone's to-do list. *I'm a data point with no return on investment. Utilitarianism has taken over the world. I'm completely screwed.*

He heard a noise, like a heavy slam, and it made him paranoid that someone was watching him. But when he looked around, all he saw were cornstalks reaching over nine feet high on both sides of the road. It must be harvest time soon, he thought. There was no one there – he'd imagined the slamming noise just like he'd imagined Gaia and Ethan talking to him last night. He'd hallucinated the whole thing, still half-drunk from downing too much guinness before bed. And now he was tens of miles from anywhere, no clue where he was, no money in his pocket, no identification, no phone that worked.

He was completely free, completely independent, and he was completely screwed. And for some reason, he was completely ecstatic. He was physically exhausted but spiritually invigorated. He imagined a young woman playing piano beside the road, simple notes, one at a time. As she spoke over the music in spanish, he listened to her and knew, even though he was hallucinating again, that he would be ok. He would be alright.

For once and for all, everything would be ok.

TWENTY NINE
long walk

It was the next morning when the first drops of rain, big and round, fell on the road. The sky was black. Thunder clapped. A bolt of lightning went to earth. Then the rain really came, pouring so heavy that Mark found himself isolated inside a shroud of water. He was soaked, his hair dripping, but he turned his face up and grinned, wondering if anyone driving past would be able to see him through the rain.

The rain came harder, pelting him for over an hour, before finally backing off to a drizzle. Mark felt exhilarated, some of his exhaustion seemed to wash away with the sweat from his body. Overhead, the black, thick clouds began to gray and thin slightly.

He was well outside the city and the suburbs, unsure how many miles he'd walked so far – at least thirty, maybe fifty. The scenery blended into a mural of woods and fields, broken by an occasional farmhouse or crossroads. He focused on going forward. But soon he would need to stop at one of these homes and ask for help, some water, some food, and a place to sleep.

He walked across an abandoned railroad track – the rails were rusty and the grass was high between the ties. He stumbled, fell, then stood up and went on walking. The rain had completely stopped and now his clothes were drying.

The rain was better than the darkness. Last night, in the cold black, morning had seemed a century away. At one point, he laid down in the grass, near a creek, to try and sleep. He drank greedily from the creek and then lay down, exhausted. But his sleep was restless; he kept imagining that he was dead, that he was buried inside the dark. He saw mourners standing around him, mourners who had walked there also, coming to see him in his tomb of blackness. After dozing in and out of his own funeral, he'd made himself get up and walk on in the dark.

I'm already going crazy. With another night like that, I could fall right off my rocker.

After the morning rain, he settled into business. *Walking and thinking,* Mark thought. *That's today's business, and the day after that, and the day after that. Walking, thinking, and embracing isolation.* He would travel in his mind while he walked with his feet. Thoughts kept coming and there was no way to stop them.

He mentally retraced his route. He'd left philadelphia around two in the morning the day before, walking on state route three. Late morning, he'd passed through a town called Goshen. His phone had died there. Then he walked due west through yesterday, last night, and today. Now he saw a sign saying he was on route three-seventy-two. The early afternoon sun told him he was headed the right direction. He'd probably get lost on the way, but no matter how lost he got on a map, he was starting to find parts of himself, way deep inside, that he hadn't even known he'd lost until now. Just walking, just being alone, just moving forward on his own two feet, just being exposed to nature, just having nothing and no idea where and how he would drink, eat, or sleep, made everything real and he embraced his dire circumstances.

His long walk continued, one step at a time. West, west, *west.* Always west. He was going to colorado, to No Law.

He walked over a wooden bridge, the planks rumbling under his feet. Mark could hear birds flapping and chattering underneath. He thought of that kid, Justin LaPointe, singing about No Law in the bar. Was that just a few weeks ago? It seemed like a thousand years…

> *I'm closing up shop, selling off my store*
> *I know this city doesn't need me no more*
> *I know it ain't no mystery*
> *I'm going on back to bear country*

This wasn't bear country – this was farm country he was in right now. Soon, he'd probably see amish, and at some point he'd see more wildlife, deer maybe. *Bear country* was a metaphor, he reminded himself. A metaphor for freedom, for untangling oneself from all the phoniness of modern life. Modern life paid well, but so did prostitution; at some point an honest man got tired of faking pleasure, no matter how well it paid. And there was even more hypocrisy required to be the pimp, which is what he'd become.

The city was killing me, now I know

<u>Now</u> *I know.* You didn't know that modern life was killing you until you were *away* from it; you couldn't see clearly until you were separate, looking back at the homicide with hindsight. He'd been lucky to escape. He'd had to go nuts to break free; his subconscious fabricating angels inside his ceiling, urging him to leave.

The hallucinations were his soul raising a red alert, getting him out of bed at two in the morning, out of the city, out of his old life, out here walking forever west so he could save himself. What would have happened if he'd stayed in bed? He would have used up Sheila and then replaced her. He would have looted another company and its employees. He would have put another billion dollars in the bank... He was done with all that. D - O - N - E. *Done.*

it'll take my body, it'll never take my soul

Luckily, enough of his soul had been intact to get him out here on the road. Now he could start rebuilding himself into the person he was supposed to be. He'd left all the nonsense behind – billions of dollars, his plane, his apartments, his houses, his companies, and Sheila. What did Sheila do when she woke up and found him gone yesterday? Did she call the police right away? Or more likely she would wait a few days, assuming he was travelling. Would the police declare him a missing person and start looking for him? Would Sheila miss him?

When it got out, the story of his disappearance would make headlines. *"Billionaire Vanishes in the Night".* He was somewhat well known, but his disappearance would make him – and Sheila – famous. In a world up for sale, the headline of a missing billionaire bachelor with a distraught supermodel girlfriend would sell a lot of clicks and commercials.

His face would be everywhere and people might be on the lookout for him, recognizing him. He needed to make himself unrecognizable. These first two days of beard, starvation, dehydration, and fatigue was a first step. Not many people would look twice at a homeless man alongside the road, most would try to avoid looking at all.

Mark looked up at the sky. It was going into early evening. He'd been walking less than two days and yet somehow it seemed like forever. He was hungry and he was tired. He imagined how nice it would be to go into a diner, settle into a booth – the relief of just sitting! – and order a burger and onion rings with an ice-cold beer; for dessert, he'd have a piece of chocolate cake and a cold glass of milk. Just a simple place to sit and eat would be heaven.

Mind over matter, he thought. *Mind over matter.* The thought became an incantation as he concentrated on making his feet rise and fall, blotting everything else out. He wasn't aware of his thirst or the steady, dull pain in his feet, or the stiffness of the muscles in his calves. A simple refrain pounded through his head like an indian drum – *walk a little longer, walk a little longer* – until the words themselves became unintelligible, meaningless sounds.

How long, Mark wondered, could a person go without sleep? without food? without water?

> *And I will walk till I fall to my knees*
> *until my heart stops, until it starts to bleed*

How long could a man endure loneliness? Live only inside his own mind, without anyone else, before he went nuts? He would get to find out. Walking alone, picking apart his soul, shining a light into the forgotten basement closets, mining the depths of Mark Halberstam. It sounded like an expedition. He would dig until he hit rock, then sledgehammer through to the true bottom. And then he would either have figured himself out, or stay trapped in the depths, never making it back up to sanity.

Walking past the farm fields, the barns, the tractors, and the animals, the satisfaction of what it must be like to live in the country settled into him. To live and work here was to do something essential – to sow and reap, to raise and care for animals, to provide food, the sustenance of life itself. It was a necessary purpose, work that everyone relied on.

He'd made his billions by siphoning wealth that others had created. He traded words, numbers, and lies for a living. He made nothing essential. If he died, no one's life would be materially different; no one would go hungry. He manipulated people and rules in a series of convolutions that, in the end, was legal theft. And while the country people lived plainly – dressed plainly, ate plainly, spoke plainly – he tried to fill his empty existence with fancy – fancy apartments, fancy suits, fancy cars, fancy restaurants, fancy vacations. Vacations from what? Not from manual labor, but to try and forget that his work failed to fulfill him.

He thought of a song that Gaia used to listen to in the kitchen. Norah Jones singing in a soft, loving voice: *Come away with me, Come away where they can't tempt us, with their lies...*

He looked at cows grazing. They chewed their cud and watched him walk past. He'd left a world of pretend, and now he was walking among the real. He could sense the difference. People living here had no illusionary corporate ladder to climb, no imaginary stock market to manipulate, no delusional hustle, no need to make a living by screwing anyone else over, no games to play while winning oscars for acting like the games were real. Out here, only hard, honest work was needed to raise food out of the ground.

He'd made his living by finding inefficiencies, removing them, and profiting from the difference. In business, inefficiency was people – salaries, pensions, healthcare benefits, time off – all inefficient. Inefficiencies could be eliminated and profits could be increased.

Efficiency. He used to throw that word around with such abandon, thinking it was always a good thing. Another great truth that was a lie. *Efficiency* had no room for faith, for a loyal one-eyed dog, for the elderly, for unwanted children. Football replaced god on sunday. The one-eyed dog was put to sleep. The elderly were put into nursing homes and fixed in front of screens. Ideally, unwanted children were aborted, or if that opportunity was missed, they were put into childcare centers to be raised by strangers. He had helped to build this efficient world, a world always striving for more efficiency, and someday it would be so efficient that no one would have to leave their homes, or their chairs, or their beds; they could just lie still, alone, looking at screens implanted behind their retinas, hooked up to feeding tubes, entertained efficiently, communicating efficiently, working efficiently – waste minimized, no unproductive time or energy. The final step to maximize efficiency would be to automate everything, eliminating people altogether.

"No efficiency!" he cried out to the sky. The rows of corn answered him by standing perfectly still. "I want wasted time and daydreaming and laziness and mistakes! I want people!"

There was some pattern to a life well lived that could not be tallied up on a profit-and-loss statement. It did not include returning value to shareholders. It did not include mergers and acquisitions. It didn't include value optimization or continuous process improvement or accelerating efficiencies.

I want to accelerate <u>inefficiencies</u>. I want to take us back to something simpler and more real, Mark thought. *I want less precision. I want to lower expectations, not raise them. I want to lose track of time and even the day of the week and not even know that I've lost track. I want to be ugly and still have people love me. I want to sit at a kitchen table for an hour and daydream, and I want to scratch a dog's belly while sitting on the grass in the sunshine.* He wanted to live like a tree, like a human tree, to be in one place and just sit and watch and think and not react quickly, but soak it all in with patience and silence, with quiet but unmovable love and commitment. Somehow, he had to slow the world down. It was spinning so fast that everyone was going to be thrown off it.

The sun was poised over the fringe of the woods, angled enough that the tall corn began to throw the road into shade. In a few hours, it would be dark and cold again. Far off to the south, Mark thought he could see purple smudges that might be more thunderheads.

He hoped it wouldn't rain during the night. Just the dark would be bad enough.

He walked west.

THIRTY
theosophy

Mark Halberstam looked up as a minivan rolled to a stop down the road. He saw someone get out of the passenger-side door and start walking toward him. His heart raced with panic; he was going to get robbed, maybe beaten or killed, and he had no strength to run or fight back. His life was near its end now anyway. His skin was sunburnt, his vision blurred, he was thirsty, exhausted, and in constant pain. He just wanted to lie down in the cool grass beside the road and rest.

The only thing that kept him walking was his certainty that if he sat down, he would never get up again. Physically, he was already dead. At this point, his body was just waiting for his mind to give in, and his mind would capitulate any minute now. He was running completely on fumes. Somewhere inside him, a final drop of adrenaline was released, a reaction to seeing the figure coming at him.

He heard sounds and woke up from his death trance to try and understand what the person was saying to him. Who was it? Another lonely walker like him? The person wasn't far now; he could see them beckoning. Mark stumbled forward. He suddenly had a vision that he and this person were the only beings alive, and that together they would be all-powerful, able to do anything, grant any wish, first wish, every wish, *death wish*. He needed to get closer so he could make out the features. Was it Ethan? Gaia? His father? His mother? Was Sheila somehow out here, walking also? Had she come for him?

A shaky groan seeped out of him. He stumbled and almost fell over on his loose legs. He had to stop; he couldn't go any further. The disappointment, the sense of loss at his death, was so staggering that it was hollow. What was the point of life? What was the point of death? What was the point of anything? He would never know.

The figure came closer, and it spoke to him. Now he could make out the words, "Yo, bro. You ok, man?"

::<>::<>::<>::<>::<>::<>::<>::<>::<>::

Truck looked at the skeleton in front of him, a man in his fifties, maybe sixties – it was impossible to tell under the filth, under the rags he wore, under the beard on his face. The man's skin was a dark brownish-red, like an indian's, and his eyes were crazed. The old man didn't speak but kept walking toward him, seemingly unafraid. He sped up slightly, lurching, alarming Truck. The old man *seemed* too weak to hurt anyone, but if he was crazy, he could do *something*. Maybe he had a weapon hidden in the torn-up rags. He was almost face-to-face with the man now and, looking closer, it seemed the rags had once been a business suit, and that the man was closer to forty than sixty.

"Yo, bro. You ok? Hey! Hey, man. You don't look good," Truck said.

"Do you…" The old man's voice trailed off. "Do you believe in the bible?"

"Um, yeah, I do. Most of it, probably."

"Yeah. Me too. I'm starting to believe in a lot of it. It's taken me awhile to get to this point. But I've made it this far." And then the man looked up at the sky with pleading eyes. Truck thought he heard a crow caw, but he looked around and didn't see any birds.

The man spun around, once, twice. "Gaia!" he cried, then he yelled, "Ethan!" Stumbling on the third spin, he fell to the ground in a heap that seemed smaller than he was when he'd been standing. Looking at the man on the ground, Truck saw a rustle of motion, a single heavy gasp, then there was no movement.

Truck bent down and said, "Hey, man. Hey, c'mon. Can you hear me?"

The man didn't move. Truck ran back to the minivan. "Come help me! This guy needs help! Get water!"

Spit and Columbus got out of the van. Spit said, "Look, we're already behind schedule. We're supposed to meet Griff in an hour, and we're at least two hours away. We *have* to be on time. We're *not* supposed to stop."

"Well, this dude is *dying!*"

"We're not a travellin' emergency room! We can't help this guy, ok? I told you not to stop!" Spit said.

"We can't just leave him here! We can't let him die!"

"Actually, we can."

"I can't. I'm not lettin' him just die on the side of the road. C'mon, help me get him into the van and give him some water. If he dies, fine. But I'm not just leavin' him."

"No. We ain't got room, and we ain't got time! I–"

"I'll make room! You can spend twenty minutes arguing with me or five minutes helpin' me. So pick 'im up!" Truck said.

"No way," Spit said, but he walked over and Columbus followed and they each reached underneath the man on the ground. He was light; they carried him and placed him on top of duffle bags in the back of the van.

"This guy's boiling," Columbus said. "Like a furnace. He's not gonna make it."

"Well, let's get goin'," Spit said. "If he dies, we're not stoppin' until we meet up with Griff. Just open the windows and let the stink out. We gotta go!"

As the minivan sped west down the country road, Truck reached back with a bottle of red gatorade. "Here," he whispered, pouring some of the red liquid onto the man's mouth, reaching with his other hand to force his lips open. The drink overflowed and dribbled onto his beard. Truck hoped that some of it leaked through the man's surprisingly white teeth and found its way into his dying body.

Spit turned up the music, and Richie Havens sang through the speakers, *"Sometimes... I feel... like a motherless child... a long... way... from my home, yeah..."* Tight guitar strums dodged between the words. Truck looked back at the dying man and tried to imagine who he was. What mistakes had forced him to torture himself this way? What had compelled him to commit slow suicide by walking alone along this nowhere road?

::<>::<>::<>::<>::<>::<>::<>::<>::<>::

Mark Halberstam woke up in pain. His head hurt, but even worse were his feet. When he moved them they felt uncoordinated and swollen. His buttocks hurt. His spine was on fire, and spasms jolted across his back with the slightest movement. But his feet were the worst. He lifted the sheets and looked down at them. They were red and swollen, the veins in his ankles bulging full of blood.

He looked around and reality crept in through the dreamish fog of waking up. A black woman sat in a chair a few feet away from him.

"Hi, sleepyhead," she said.

Mark tried to smile. He examined her face, but he didn't recognize her.

"You're ok," she said. "Just rest. You're very tired, but I think maybe you'll be ok."

"Who are you? Where am I?"

"The king's castle inn, near rockford, illinois. West of peoria. They found you on the road a few hours east of here. Lookin' bad. We brought you here to rest. I'm Maggie."

"Why didn't you take to me a hospital?"

"We might take you to a hospital. We haven't decided yet."

"Who's we?"

"There's a group of us travelling together. Don't worry. I don't think anyone's going to hurt you. If they wanted to hurt you, they could have left you back there to die."

Mark searched his mind. He didn't know who this woman was or how he got here, but memories started coming back. Illinois, she'd said, west of peoria. He was farther west now. He clearly remembered indiana, walking along route twenty-four. Before that? He'd caught a ride with a farmer in shrewsbury, pennsylvania. Then he'd walked and bummed rides into and across ohio. Somewhere in ohio, a bar band travelling to chicago for a gig picked him up. They'd been driving an old ford econoline van with ohio plates, a pair of electric guitars painted on the sides, their necks crossed like swords, along with the name of the group: *GARD AND THE*

TOMMYKNOCKERS. When the van pulled over, Mark had run to it, panting, with pain pulsing in his back and calves. In spite of the pain, he'd been amused by the words lettered across the van's doors: "IF GARD'S ROCKIN', DON'T COME KNOCKIN'".

Four bandmates were in the van, and his arrival made it a tight fit. The interior was crammed with musical instruments, amplifiers, cords, and stands. The gaps were stuffed with assorted blankets, pillows, and duffel bags. Everything was packed densely, squeezing all the passengers together.

They introduced themselves. Gard was driving. Steve was riding shotgun. Kish, the bassist, mumbled his name gloomily while leaning against the back window and half-dozing. Mark clearly remembered the only woman in the van, Tabitha. She was young, wore cutoff denim jeans, and she laughed a lot. She gave him a bottle of water and kept passing him lit joints whenever he woke up. Her roach clip was a colorfully beaded bobby pin that maybe came from her punk-cut, dyed-red hair.

"Guaranteed to kill all bad dreams," Tabitha had said solemnly to him at one point, handing him a lit marijuana cigarette after he'd woken himself up by talking in his sleep, worried about what he'd said out loud. *The worst dreams never die, beautiful,* he thought. *Take it from me. Some nightmares are eternal.*

He'd told them his name was Gabe Dismas – he remembered his grade school misfit friend and loved the name. It was his travelling name, he decided, a name he could be proud of because it had no reputation, no history of homicidal lust and betrayal associated with it, as far as he knew.

He'd taken small hits off the joint for politeness' sake, and each time his head swam at once. At one point, he handed the dope back to the girl, who was sitting against the van's sliding door, and said, "I really need something to eat."

'Got a box of ritz crackers," Gard had said and handed it back. "We ate everything else. Steve even ate the *sardines*. Sorry."

"Steve'd eat anything," Tabi said.

Steve looked back at them. He was skinny, with dark hair, wearing thick glasses, with a wide, pleasant face. "Untrue," he said. "*Un*true. I'd *never* eat your boogers."

They all laughed. Mark said, "The crackers are fine. Thanks." And they were. He'd eaten slowly at first, then faster and faster, until he was gobbling the crackers in handfuls, his stomach snarling for more.

Now, lying there in the king's castle inn, he wondered if he had eaten anything since that delicious box of crackers. When had he last eaten? Oh, yeah, the roadside restaurant after Gard had dropped him off. After that, he didn't know. It was lost in the blackout of endless walking.

"Mister, you sure you're alright?" Tabitha had asked him at another point. He remembered noticing that her legs went approximately up to her breasts.

"Yeah, don't I look alright?"

"No," she'd answered gravely. That had made him smile – not what she'd said, but the seriousness with which she'd said it – and she'd smiled back at him.

The band had picked him up in the early morning and they dropped him off in the early evening, so he must have slept a long time, dozing between tokes from the beaded bobby-pin roach clip, drinking water, and eating the entire box of ritz crackers. He'd told Gard he'd ride along while they headed west, and when they turned north to chicago, he'd get out. Gard had woken him up to tell him he was getting on interstate sixty-five soon. He'd drop Mark off before they got on. Mark had looked out the window and seen that the clouds were columns of scales, merging into a solid gray that looked like a brewing storm. When they dropped him off, it would be dark and probably raining. Sure enough, right as the van pulled over to let him out, the first drops of water were plopping on the windshield.

"Listen, Gabe," Gard said, pulling over, "I hate to leave you here. It's starting to rain and you don't even have a raincoat."

"I'll be ok."

"You don't look so ok," Tabitha said softly.

Gard whipped off his hat – DON'T BLAME ME I VOTED FOR TED THE POWER MAN was written over the visor – and put five bucks in it, then said, "Cough it up, c'mon." Wallets appeared; change jingled.

"No! Hey, thanks, but no!" Mark felt blood rush into his cheeks in embarrassment. *Okay,* he thought. *You've heard people talk about hitting rock bottom. This is what it feels like. Here it is. Mark Halberstam, the great american tycoon, taking handouts from an ohio bar band.*

"Really, no—"

Gard went on passing the hat just the same until it contained a few paper bills and some change. Kish got the hat last and tossed in a dollar.

"Look," Mark said, "I appreciate it, but—"

"C'mon, Kish," Gard said. "Cough up, you stinge."

"Really, I have friends. I'll just call a few up—" Mark added wildly.

"Kish is a stinge," Tabitha began to chant gleefully, *"Kish is a stinge, Kish is a stinge!"*

The others had picked it up until Kish, laughing and rolling his eyes, added two quarters, a five-dollar bill, and a powerball lottery ticket. "There, I'm tapped," he said, "unless you want some good lovin'." Everyone laughed wildly. Gard tossed the hat to Mark who had to catch it; otherwise, the money would have fallen all over the floor.

"Really," he'd said, trying to give the hat back to Gard. "I'm okay. Please. I don't want your money." He was embarrassed and humiliated.

"You *ain't* okay," Gard said. "So take it, pay it forward later. What do you say?"

"Thanks. Thank you all." He took the bills and change and put them in his pocket, handing a slip of white paper back to Gard. "Keep the lottery ticket, just in case that lovin' thing doesn't work out."

Gard took the ticket and laughed, "Well, it ain't so much you'll have to pay taxes on it. But it'll buy you some burgers."

Tabitha slid open the van's sidewall door. "Get better, understand?" she said and handed him a water bottle. Then, before he could reply, she hugged him and gave him a kiss, her mouth friendly, half-open, lingering, and reminiscent of pot. "Take care."

"I'll try." On the verge of getting out, he suddenly hugged her again, fiercely, clinging to her. "Thank you."

He'd stood at the end of the ramp and seen his shadow in the lights of a gas station, a restaurant, passing semi-trucks, and cars. The rain had started falling more steadily, and he watched as the van's sidewall door rumbled shut on its track. The girl waved just before it closed. Mark waved back, and then the van rolled down the interstate breakdown lane, gathering speed, finally merging into the travel lane.

Mark had watched them go, one hand still raised in a wave in case they (*she?*) might be looking back, tears running freely down his cheeks, mixing with the rain. After that, he'd gotten a delicious dinner at the restaurant then walked along state route twenty-four through indiana into illinois, getting lost in a straight-line maze of endless fields, rows of corn after rows of corn after rows of corn.

He thought about the band – Gard, Steve, Tabitha, and Kish. They gave freely to him despite their poverty. They'd given from what they themselves needed. He'd never done that. He'd always donated from his abundance; he'd always donated in exchange for the tax deduction, favors, and recognition: the sponsored gallery, the hospital plaque, his name listed in the theatre program. The band was broke and homeless themselves – living on sardines, ritz crackers, and pot – and yet they gave him the last of their money.

And now he was again the beneficiary of the kindness of strangers. This black woman, Maggie, and the people with her, had taken him in and given him a place to rest. They saved his life. *Why?* What was in it for them? What was the scam? Had he ever helped a homeless person in his life? *No.* Had he ever contemplated giving without getting? *Never.*

A few days ago, he'd been a billionaire playboy, but that man was a different person, a man he'd heard about, someone lodged in his memory, but completely distinct from himself. Out here, on the road, he was being reborn. His old life was gone. He had new wisdom. He now saw a new path; and maybe it led to salvation.

He looked at the woman, Maggie. She looked at him and asked, "What's your name?"

He reminded himself what to say. "Gabe Dismas," he said, and smiled.

"How are you feeling?" Maggie asked him.

"Better. Absolutely horrible, but better."

Maggie laughed. "Well, you couldn't get any *worse*. You're in such bad shape you can *only* get better." She handed him a glass of water from the nightstand. "Here, drink this."

Mark sipped the water, and his thirst suddenly came to life, surprising him. He finished the first glass and then two more that she brought him. After he finished the last glass of water, he lay back, closed his eyes, and heard her say, "Just rest now, Gabe. Just sleep for a while."

"Ok. Good idea," Mark said. And he slept.

::<>::<>::<>::<>::<>::<>::<>::<>::<>::

"Hey, boss," Spit said. "I think this might be the guy that everyone's lookin' for. That billionaire that disappeared."

"What are you talkin' about?"

"Mark Halberstam, he's a rich wall street guy who disappeared like a week ago. Look." He handed Griffin his phone.

Griffin Turner looked at the screen and scrolled with his thumb. "This does look a lot like him. But all these white guys look the same."

Spit laughed. "Here, check this video out. Give me the phone." Griffin handed the phone back. Spit tapped, scrolled, then handed the device back to Griffin with a video playing. A man was speaking to a reporter.

"Wow, that's his wife with him?"

"Girlfriend. Sheila McPherson. She's a super-hot supermodel. Sports illustrated last year. His wife and four kids died in the new york city nuking in may. They're charcoal."

"That would drive someone nuts."

"Yeah. Maybe that's why he disappeared. His girlfriend says he's losing it – drinking all the time, disappearing alone for days. He was crying a lot for no reason. She said he was talking to people who weren't there. He was hallucinating people and animals talking to him."

"This says he's worth over twenty billion dollars. Wow. A lotta people are tryin' to find him."

"Yeah or get their paws on his money."

"What room's he in?"

"Three-thirty-two. Sleeping. Maggie's checkin' on him. He's already a lot better. I think he's good enough for us to leave 'im. I hope we're leaving him. This guy, and all of 'em, is exactly what we're tryin' to get away from."

"Yeah. Yeah. But look, I mean, maybe we can do business with this guy. We helped him out, he helps us out? We need money, Spit. We got some, but between you and me, it's not enough. No one coughed up what they were supposed to. I don't know how this is all goin' to work out, but every dollar we got gives us a better chance. We need serious cash. Right now, we only have enough to get us into colorado. To get a lot of good land and get set up takes money we don't got. I've been lookin' hard for some answer – I've even been *prayin'* for one. Maybe this dude is it. This insane, half-dead, bible-babblin' billionaire walkin' alone and dyin' on the highway."

"Well, we're not even positive it's him. Why don't you talk to him and find out?"

"Should I wake him up? I'm thinkin' let him sleep."

"Yeah, let him sleep. Talk to him tonight, or tomorrow morning when he's more rested. I mean, he's gettin' stronger physically, but he still seems out of it mentally, you know?"

"Is he still talkin' about the bible all the time?"

"A lot of the time. It's weird. Everythin' he says is crazy, but he pulls you in until you're sort of on the same page with him. I know everythin' he says is whacko, but part of me is agreein' with him at the same time."

"Yeah, yeah. The bible'll do that to you. It's all nonsense you can never ignore for some reason. Why *is that*, man? Is it 'cause they bake it into us so early that it's just crusted in there, residue that won't ever fully scrape away? Or is it 'cause there's some kind of truth to all of it? Some truth we can't just ignore because somethin' inside us, put there before we were born, knows it's true, if we can finally fit the puzzle pieces together?"

"I don't know, boss. It's a good question to ask this dude, Gabe Dismas or Mark Halberstam or whoever he is. It seems like he's askin' a lot of the same questions. Maybe *he's* got some answers."

"Yeah. Ok. Tell Maggie to get me when he wakes up and I'll talk to him."

THIRTY ONE
resurrection

Mark Halberstam woke up. At least, he thought he was awake. His dreams had been so lucid that for a few moments he wondered if he was waking up inside a dream. And maybe that dream was inside another dream. Maybe dreams were as real as any other reality. Was the imaginary as real as what he truly saw and heard? Maybe nothing was real, so everything was.

Maybe every life was a Philip K. Dick story, where answers were first found to be phony, but then later revealed to be truth. "Everything is true. Everything anybody has ever thought," was the last communication from bounty hunter Rick Deckard in Dick's book, *Do Androids Dream of Electric Sheep?* At the end of the book, Deckard had found a toad, turned it over, saw an on/off switch, and realized that the animal was phony, a machine. And yet something real made the phony; reality was required to design and manufacture the fake, and so the phony was *real*. The idea was as real as the physical, the word as real as the deed, the dream life as real as the waking life.

Mark thought of Jesus. Somehow he had to reconcile these concepts with Christ's words from the bible. He leaned over, opened the hotel nightstand drawer, and picked up the red-bound book there. *HOLY BIBLE* was inscribed on the red cover in gold letters. *PLACED BY THE GIDEONS* was below it, in smaller type. He opened the book and read the first passage that appeared, Matthew, chapter five, verse eighteen: "For truly I say to you, until heaven and earth pass away, not the smallest letter or stroke shall pass from the Law until all is accomplished."

Until all is accomplished...

What must be accomplished? Mark wondered.

ALL

He picked another random page and read Luke, chapter twenty-one, verse thirty-two: "Truly I say to you, this generation will not pass away until all things take place."

Until all things take place… All things…

ALL

How can all things take place? Mark wondered. Jesus is saying that all realities will be experienced, and if that is true, then there's nothing to be afraid of because everything must happen. Everyone must be scared, must be horny, must love, hate, kill, conceive, be born, die, be confused, know everything, know nothing. It *all* must be accomplished. It *all* must take place.

It seemed impossible that every conceivable moment could occur. *But within eternity,* Mark thought, *with no end to time, it's entirely possible. And if we are all part of god, of a singular consciousness, then we could, given infinite time, experience everything.* The truth started to become clear to him when he abandoned the concepts of time and individuality.

He opened the bible to a different page and read romans, chapter twelve, verse five: "So we, who are many, are one body in Christ, and individually members of one another."

And now I know the truth, Mark thought. That everything is the truth, and it doesn't matter if people believe me because them not believing me is part of the truth, and it doesn't matter if I'm killed because my death is part of the truth. I will be poor, I will be rich, I will be virtuous, I will sin. I'm always living a moment of an eternal collective existence that encompasses every possibility, and so every act is justified. I'm god and everyone is god and we are all one. Our uniqueness and individuality are imaginary but necessary so that every truth can be lived, including the truth of ignorance and false separation.

The same man who was the chief executive officer of an international corporation was the same woman who was a pregnant unwed mother, Mark thought. We are all Christ, hanging from a cross, covered in blood and sweat; and we are all Lucifer, raping and ripping apart and killing; and we are all god, creating and giving birth and sharing our eternal wisdom; and we are all love, the holy spirit itself, encompassing everything. I've evolved, Mark thought. I now know that there is not a trinity, rather there is a *quaternity*, four entities within everything that exists. The first is love and joy, also called the holy spirit; the second is persistence and suffering, also called Christ; the third is wisdom and creativity, god himself; and finally, there is Lucifer – evil and ignorance. Each part of the quaternity is holy.

Every moment of existence includes one or more of these four realities, Mark thought. Until now, Lucifer was thought to be separate, and so we've always felt separate from god. But now he saw that evil was as necessary as love, suffering, and wisdom.

He heard the door unlatch and open, and he looked up from the bible. "Hey there, sleepyhead," a woman said – Maggie, he remembered. She had a kind, beautiful face.

"Hi," Mark said.

"How are you feeling?"

"Much better. I'm hungry. But good. Thank you for taking care of me."

"You're welcome. Here's some fruit and some milk, stuff from the free breakfast this morning." She put a paper plate with a banana, an apple, and a cardboard carton of milk on it next to the nightstand. "Have at it. And my husband, Griffin, wants to talk with you, ok? You two can figure out what to do next, before we say goodbye."

Mark leaned over, picked up the banana, and started peeling it. "Sure, that's great. Thanks for the food. Whenever he wants to talk is fine."

"Ok, I'll let him know."

::<>::<>::<>::<>::<>::<>::<>::<>::<>::

"He's ready, Griff," Maggie said. "He's awake and eating. I told him I was coming to get you."

"Ok, babe." Griffin hugged her, holding on for an extra moment. "Thanks," he said as she handed him the room card.

Griffin walked down the hall, entered room three-thirty-two, and saw Gabe Dismas sitting up in bed, eating an apple, the bible open on his lap. Gabe looked up at him.

"Hi, I'm Griffin, Maggie's husband."

"Hi, Griffin, I'm Gabe Dismas," Mark Halberstam said. "Maggie's really nice. I really appreciate everything you've done to help me. Thank you. I would have died without your help."

"Yeah," Griffin laughed. He held out his hand and said, "You're welcome. How are you doing now?"

Mark turned to sit with his feet off the side of the bed; he shook Griffin's hand and replied, "Ok. Just resting, eating. I keep feeling better."

"So what happened to put you out there on the road?"

"I'm heading west. Walking and bumming rides. I'm trying to go to colorado."

"No Law. Why?"

"I need to start over. Somewhere that I'm free."

"Most people drive, my man. Maybe fly, or take a train. Or a bus."

"Listen, I took a greyhound from boston to new york city once. It was a... *bad experience*. I'd *crawl* before I'd take the bus."

Griffin laughed. "Well, you were just about crawlin'. It must have been a real lousy bus ride."

"I'm still not sure what I'm doing," Mark said, feeling tears come to his eyes. "I just know I couldn't keep doing what I *was* doing. I had to leave. I have to start over in colorado. I heard this kid singing in a bar about No Law, then I saw Declan Kikas on television talking about it, then I had this dream where my family talked to me. I was in bed in the middle of the night and some switch flipped in my mind. I left and took nothing with me and just started walking west."

"There must be some logical reason," Griffin said. "Either that or you've gone insane."

"Maybe I'm insane. But if so, I already was. I killed my entire family and I can't get over that. I can never pay for that. So instead, I have to become a different person so I'm no longer guilty. I have to be born again, like the bible talks about."

"How did *you* kill them? I read they died in the terrorist attacks."

"*Wait.* How did you know that?"

"You're Mark Halberstam, right? You're not Gabe Dismas. You're the billionaire who disappeared?"

"You know me?"

"You're in the news, my friend. Your girlfriend reported you missing. I saw your picture, your girlfriend's picture – she's stunning, by the way. I'm not sure how any man can leave *that*."

Mark laughed. "Yeah. That's another thing I have to get away from – *her*, yes, but all women entirely. They... distort my thinking. I lose the ability to be rational, logical, moral."

"Well, colorado won't fix that problem. There's women there too."

"Yeah. But out here, walking alone, at least I've been able to clear my head of them. I've been able to figure things out without the distraction. I've had to physically separate myself from everyone and everything I know so I can start over without my thoughts being distorted."

"How did you kill your family?"

"I'll tell you and you'll be the third person alive who knows. My wife and kids and I were supposed to leave manhattan before the blasts. I asked them to stay in the city an extra day so I could have another night with Sheila, that model, in the caribbean. They stayed and died because of me. A lot of people probably think I've just recently lost my mind, but I lost it long ago, well before I ever killed my family, and now I'm trying to find out what sanity is, what being a good person is. I've got to get to No Law and there I'll be free to find out. It's some combination of myself, the bible, and nature that I have to piece together. I'm going to colorado and I'm starting completely over."

"Yeah," Griffin said. "Well, we're going there to start over too. There's forty of us."

Mark looked at Griffin and thought of Gard and his band, *the Tommyknockers*, coughing up their spare change and their last box of ritz crackers to help him, a stranger. Griffin and Maggie, these people also had helped him only because it was the right thing to do, with no thought of themselves.

When have I done something selfless?

Never. But it was time. It was his turn to help others, to do something good for no reason than because it was good. "I've got billions of dollars. I'll give it to you and maybe you let me come with you."

"Look," Griffin said, "we need the money for sure. But if we got some rich guy everyone's lookin' for with us, it just complicates things. It just adds another huge problem to my list. I don't know what you're up to. I don't know what you're all about. I don't know how you work under pressure. My friends that helped you, they're all my brothers and sisters lookin' for a new, free life on our own, without relyin' on anyone else. What I want is freedom. And I don't get it by relyin' on anyone."

"I see it as *me* relying on *you*, ok? I don't want to slow you down. Or interfere with what you're doing. I could keep travelling alone. But if I'm going the same way, I could help you like you've helped me."

"I'm done with people helping me. Done expecting help. Our plan – our dream – is to get into No Law and take care of ourselves or die tryin'. And the plan don't include you. That's nothing personal."

"Look, you don't understand," Mark said. "I need to do something good, like you did for me, picking me up and taking care of me, saving my life. Like you're doing leading your friends to freedom."

"*No charity*. Don't you understand? Yeah, we need the money. But I'm *sick* of being *helped!* I want to do it on my own! I'm going to be a man for the first time in my life. If I fail, *I* fail – not the system or the government or anyone else but *me*. If we succeed, it's going to be on our *own*, without havin' to thank anyone."

"Ok, let's just do business together then. One mile at a time, one day at a time. You decide how far, but I'm going to No Law too, to start over. I'm changing my name and starting over where the past has disappeared, where the future is all there is. Take me along one day at a time, and when either of us gets tired of the other, we can push the eject button and say goodbye. If you got bank account info, I'll get online right now and move money to you. It's yours because none of its mine. A different man made all that money. It doesn't belong to me anymore. Every dollar I make from now on is going to be honest, which probably means I'll be broke," Mark laughed.

"You don't get it. You–"

"Look, it's not charity if I'm paying you for a ride and protection. For food and water. When I did it on my own. I almost died. You saved my life. You said I should take a plane or a bus? Well, I'd pay them. And there's no one who would help get me past the federal checkpoints going into No Law. If I was in a hospital, I'd be paying doctor bills. If I was living my old life, I'd be paying for my sins with my immortal soul. A billion dollars is cheap by comparison. If I go out there on the road alone again, I'll die. I'm paying you for my life, for a ride and for protection, as far as you want to take me."

"Do you know how to farm? To raise animals? To live off the land?"

"No. Hah, no way. My wife used to garden at our country place and I helped her a few times. Do you?"

"We're going to learn. We got books. We got a lot of tools."

"Well, if you got a lot of money, it gives you more time to learn. There's more room for making mistakes."

"It's funny… each of us lives in entirely different worlds – you rich with everything, me poor with nothin', stealin' and dealin' to survive – and yet neither of us has any idea how to make an honest livin' on our own, away from society. If you come with us, you gotta understand that you're low man on the totem pole. If there's a dirty, dangerous job to do, you're goin' to do it. If we run out of water, you're goin' thirsty. If we run out of food–

"I'm gonna starve–"

"No," Griffin laughed, "we're gonna *eat* you so *we* don't starve. You *diggin' it,* dude? We're bringin' you along because you're paying us and will work for us. When we need room, you're the one riding with his legs piled full of stuff. Get it?"

"Yeah, yeah, I get it, Griffin. Just let me come with you."

"I need to talk with everyone, see what they think."

"Before you talk to them, can you get a laptop? And your bank account info. I want you to show them something."

"Ok." Griffin left and came back a few minutes later with a laptop that he handed to Mark.

Mark started typing and said, "Here, put in your bank account number and nine-digit routing number."

Griffin took the device and looked at the glowing screen. "Wow," he said. He looked up the numbers on his phone, typed them in, and handed it back to Mark.

"This is just the beginning."

"This is more than enough," Griffin laughed.

"Well, it should do for a start to help convince your friends."

Griffin laughed again. "Jesus holy Christ."

"If Jesus had this much money," Mark laughed, "he could have chartered a yacht instead of walking." He clicked a button on the screen and handed the laptop back. "There. You're worth a hundred million bucks. You're in the top one percent of the one percent. Do you feel any different?"

"Yeah. I feel like a lot of problems and worries just disappeared."

"It's a very real feeling, even though it's all imaginary, right? Nothing's changed, but now you feel different, even though everything is the same. I mean, I could cancel the wire transfer and nothing physically would change. My grandma would visit my mansions and say, 'Mark, you can only stand in one room at time.' She annoyed me because she was always right."

Griffin laughed. "I'll be back," he said.

::<>::<>::<>::<>::<>::<>::<>::<>::<>::

Griffin met with Maggie and his twelve men, and it was an easy decision. Everyone sat stupefied with dazed smiles, shocked and unable to fully process the miracle that had happened.

Couch spoke and summed it up for all of them. "Griff, go tell him he's got a deal before he comes to his senses."

THIRTY TWO
borderline

Let me be a free man, free to travel, free to stop,
free to work, free to trade where I choose,
free to choose my own teachers,
free to follow the religion of my fathers,
free to talk, think, and act for myself.

— Chief Joseph

Griffin Turner looked around the cheap motel room in big springs, nebraska. Some men were sitting on the queen bed. Some leaned against the plasterboard wall while others sat on the wine colored carpet. Gabe Dismas, formerly known as Mark Halberstam, sat on the floor near the window. Maggie sat in a plastic swiveling chair near the television.

Griffin said, "We're close to the colorado border, just a few miles away from No Law. This is the most dangerous part of our journey. We need to try and figure out how to get past the federal checkpoints."

Cig said, "I got real bad feelings. They got guns and we got guns."

Griffin said, "I hear you. I'm worried too. So today, Couch and Jocelyn and their kids went to two border checkpoints. First, state route one-thirty-eight, then interstate seventy-six, to see what they look like and what happens when you try to get in. They told the guards they're on vacation because we heard people can get a special permit to go in on vacation, so they tried. They checked things out."

"Let's hear it, Couch," Truck said.

Couch leaned against the wall, he looked around the room while he spoke,

"From what I saw today, we're not gettin' into colorado without lightin' people up. The two border crossings that Jocelyn and I cased are set up like stateville, like *maximum security*, man. And the feds are antsy. They had guns out and pointed at us the second time and I think the only reason they let us reverse outta there is 'cause we had the kids with us. We hit route one-thirty-eight first, the two-lane state route, and it was beefed up at the crossing with barb-wire fence thirty feet high in both directions along the border, as far as the eye could see. It was all concrete, guns, military vehicles, police vehicles; there's nothin' nice and easy about it. They got it all locked down tight. I drove and Jossy recorded it on her phone so you can watch the video.

"The soldiers at the first checkpoint wanted to know if we were citizens and why we wanted in. I told 'em vacation and they said no way. They were pretty nice about it and just let us go back. Then we tried at the interstate checkpoint. It was just as built up, with feronia soldiers, concrete barriers, barbed wire, and dogs – bomb-sniffin' dogs, drug-sniffin' dogs, automatic weapons–"

Truck interrupted, "This sounds crazy. It's like colorado's become a different country."

Couch continued, "They knew who we were and that we'd just tried to cross on one thirty-eight. They were suspicious and angry. They had us pull over to a side lane, they questioned us and searched the van. While we were there, about six other vehicles come up. Four of 'em showed papers and were let through; the other two got questioned and were turned away. I saw four cars drive *out* of colorado, and they were briefly stopped leavin', then waved on into nebraska. There were about ten soldiers at the route one-thirty-eight two-lane checkpoint, about twenty working the interstate crossin'.

"There's news media and anti-government protesters camped out on the No Law side of the border at both spots. Tents set up and protesters got drones flyin' and cameras out and signs set up. They're filmin' everything, and they yelled and waved signs whenever anyone got turned away from comin' through. All the protesters I could see had guns – holsters on their hips, rifles and assault weapons slung over their shoulders."

"So whaddaya think we should do, Couch?" Griffin asked.

"I don't see how to get through peacefully, Griff," Couch answered. "They were really aggressive the second time, tore the car apart looking for god knows what and had the dogs sniff through everythin'. Once you're pulled over into their holdin' area, you're facing concrete barriers all around you, you're stuck, so we *can't* let 'em move us into there because you can only barely reverse out of there."

Wood said, "I think we all line up close together. There's eight minivans and the two u-hauls with all forty-one of us. Whoever's first tells 'em we're all together and we're goin' in, seekin' political asylum from the incarcerated states of america. We want peaceful and safe passage into the republic of colorado. If they hesitate or try to pull us over, we raise the gun barrels, hit the gas, and charge through. If they shoot first, we shoot back. And we don't stop until we're sixty or a hundred miles in, maybe all the way to denver."

"Do we go through the two-lane or the interstate?" Fish asked.

"Interstate," Couch said. "There's more feds, but there's also more protestors and cameras and drones watching everythin'. If they try anythin' too crazy, there'll be witnesses. If they try to chase us into colorado, I think those protesters on the No Law side might even light up any feds tryin' to follow us."

"Maybe we have to shoot," Griffin said. "But I hope not. We're gonna try and do it peaceful. We won't hurt anyone unless we have to. We won't shoot unless they shoot first."

"They'll shoot. That's what they do. They're looking for any excuse," Club said.

Griffin said, "Look, guns are an option, but so is just passin' through without having to fire. All we want is safe passage. If they give us that, we're good. If they don't, then yeah, we'll kill as many of 'em as we have to, blow 'em all away if we need to. They chose to put that uniform on; they took a vow to protect citizens and to protect freedom. Will they really try to kill citizens who are just tryin' to live free?"

Cig said, "If so, hellfire's gonna rain down on 'em. 'I'm full of the fury of the lord,' as old Sam used to say."

"Old Sam! *The* man!" P-rock exclaimed.

"The myth and the legend!" someone else said. Everyone laughed.

"When do we go?" Mini asked.

"Day after tomorrow," Griffin said. "At dawn. First light. They got night vision so they got an unfair advantage in the dark. We'll go just before sunrise, the day after tomorrow."

"The dawn of a new day," Couch said. "We'll make our stand as the sun rises, just as first light touches upon the promised land, our sanctuary in No Law."

"Hell yeah," a voice added.

Wood said, "Make sure all your phones are charged, and that you got chargers in the front seat of each van. Test the push-to-talk apps on each phone. At least two phones per vehicle for whoever is shotgun. We need to be in constant communication. I wanna do a full comms test before we go. And we need to rehearse different scenarios. No one fires unless fired upon *or* you get the command from Griffin or me."

Gabe Dismas sat quietly against the wall, his eyes downcast towards the cheap carpet, his left leg jittering slightly. *This is going to be a bloodbath,* he thought. *There will be a gunfight at the colorado border.* He closed his eyes. His stomach dropped low, down to somewhere in his thighs, his lungs tightened, and he struggled to breathe calmly. He was scared. *What have I gotten myself into? This is a bunch of ex-con criminals and I'm with them, the feds will kill us all without thinking twice; we're going to war with the most powerful government in the world. Crossing alive is a fantasy, they're going to kill all of us, they're going to kill me. I'm going to die. I'm going to die. None of us will make it into No Law alive. I have to back out of this, just disappear and wander off on my own. I thought I wanted to start over in No Law, but I could start over anywhere, go to california or mexico, somewhere where they aren't trying to kill me on my way in.*

"Everyone needs to wear their armored vests – hide 'em under your shirts," Wood said. "Make sure the weapons and all the extra clips are loaded and close at hand."

Griffin said, "We're gonna list out a chain of command and text it to everyone. If I die, Wood's in charge. If Wood's gone, then Spit, then Couch, and so on. I'll send everyone a text with it."

Griffin continued, "Ok. Let's call it a night. Everyone get a good night's sleep. We need to rest up. This is getting real. Listen to me, all of you. We've lived lies for so long that the truth is scary, but we're done bowin' down to any other man. Some of us might die or get left behind when we cross over, but they will be martyrs for the rest of us who make it to freedom, so our children can live in truth. All of you get ready for it. And all of you be brave."

THIRTY THREE
running men

The Lockheed struck the Games Building dead on, three quarters of the way up.
Its tanks were still better than a quarter full.
Its speed was slightly over five hundred miles an hour.
The explosion was tremendous, lighting up the night like the wrath of God,
and it rained fire twenty blocks away.

— Richard Bachman, *The Running Man*

"Ok, y'all," Griffin Turner's voice came across the push-to-talk application on everyone's phones. "Here we go. We gotta fight to live. We gotta struggle now. Fight to live. I know most of you have never done anything like this before. Some of us might die. Some of our kids might die. That's the way it will be. We gotta fight to live."

Griffin rode shotgun in the lead minivan as Maggie drove. Gabe sat in the rear seat behind Griffin, and Spit sat behind Maggie; both men had assault rifles at their feet, with clips of ammunition and more guns on the floor between them.

Griffin spoke into his phone, "Here we go. This is where slavery ends and freedom begins. This is where we're washed clean of our sins and start to live pure. This is where we're born again. This is where it gets real. Here we go. Heads held high, guns held low, be ready to bring 'em up. We're headed into freedom. We will sit on thrones. All for one. None of us could do this on our own, but together, it's gonna happen. We're headed into the promised land. We will rule ourselves. And never forget that I love each and every one of you."

They made their way down interstate seventy-six. It was minutes past six in the morning when they rounded a bend and saw the roadblock in the distance. About a thousand yards from the colorado border was a blue sign with white letters and an arrow pointing to the leftmost lane. The sign said:

<u>READY LANE</u>
Travelers w/ Prior Authorization Enter Here

"Get all the way left, Maggie," Griffin said. Then he spoke into his phone, "Everyone take the ready lane. Stay left."

Maggie merged into the left lane, then stopped the minivan in front of a sign that said:

<u>STOP HERE UNTIL SIGNALED FORWARD</u>

<u>BE PREPARED TO SHOW IDENTIFICATION</u>

<u>WARNING!</u>
If you enter Colorado without presenting yourself to a Border Officer
YOU MAY BE ARRESTED AND PROSECUTED
For Violating U.S. Immigration and Customs Laws

Up ahead they could see fences, concrete barriers, and barbed wire. There were soldiers clad in bulletproof vests and helmets wearing wraparound sunglasses. They had handguns holstered on each thigh, rifles hung over their shoulders, earbuds in their ears, and microphones on their helmet chinstraps. Surveillance cameras recorded activity from every angle. Spotlights were mounted on poles. Everything at the border was emotionless – digital and mechanical.

The morning was very bright and everything was very sharp and clearly defined. At the checkpoint ahead of them, two soldiers spoke to a gray-haired man in an old pickup and then waved it through. As the truck drove into colorado, a soldier holding a clipboard waved them forward.

Griffin spoke into his phone, "This is Griff. It's startin'. Ok, y'all, be lined up. Lock the doors. Cameras rolling everyone. I want this whole thing recorded and live-streamed from each vehicle. No one fires unless fired upon or until you get my signal."

Griffin looked at Maggie and said, "Drive up to him and stop."

Here we go, Gabe thought. *Oh dear god, here we go.*

Maggie rolled the minivan forward slowly. Soldiers wearing olive-green fatigues stood on each side of the white painted lanes, black metal guns holstered on each hip.

"Are these local or feronia?" Maggie asked.

"All feds it looks like," Griffin answered. "Lock the doors and bring your window down. Be ready to slam it into drive and start moving. Spit and Gabe, be ready to open it up."

Griffin spoke into the phone, "This is Griff. Be ready. Be ready to blitz if I give the word."

Answers crackled back from the vehicles lined up behind them, "Ok." ... "Got it." ... "Roger that." ... "We're good."

Maggie stopped just in front of the soldier who had waved her forward. The soldier glanced inquiringly at her and came to her window. The second soldier stood at Griffin's window. A third soldier, who'd been sitting in a glass booth with his feet up, came outside the booth and stood to watch them.

"How're you guys doing?" the first soldier asked.

"Good," Maggie said.

"Are you all united states citizens?"

"Yes sir, we are," Maggie answered.

"Are you colorado residents?"

"No sir, we're from illinois," Maggie said.

"Ok. Can you please pull over into that lane over there?"

"Is there a problem, sir?" Griffin asked.

"Yeah, there is. I'm sure you've heard. No nonresidents are allowed into colorado. Even the licensed tourist exemption was revoked. So if you don't have a government card from feronia, you can't go into the state. Do you have any weapons, cash, agricultural items like plants, fruits, and vegetables? Any animals?"

"Yeah, yeah to most of that, except no animals with us," Griffin said.

"Are all these vehicles back there with you? You all together?"

"Yeah," Griffin answered.

"Well, you all need to pull over there," the soldier said, pointing to Maggie's right. "None of you people are coming in here."

"What's all *those* people doing on the other side?" Griffin asked, pointing past the border checkpoint. Gabe looked ahead. On the other side of the border were clusters of people, some with signs, some sitting on camp chairs in front of tents. He saw three drones in a stable hover above the group. A man in a black sweatshirt, jeans, and dark sunglasses held up a sign in one hand that said, "Unjust Law is NO LAW at All". His other hand held a styrofoam cup. He had a rifle slung over his shoulder.

"They're upset. Rebels and protesters saying all these checkpoints in and out of colorado are unconstitutional."

"*Is* this constitutional? I don't think it is," Griffin said.

"That question is way above my pay grade. We just stop the traffic coming through the border and only let authorized vehicles and people in."

"I still don't understand the problem. We aren't doin' anything wrong."

"Yeah, sorry sir. Look, only people on official business are allowed to enter colorado. You need permission from the united states government to come in."

"So you're lettin' some people in?" Griffin asked.

"Just residents with a permit, or some credentialed press or government people. But if you're not a current resident of colorado, you're not getting in. Now the rules keep changing. I mean, just a couple weeks ago they were looser, letting tourists in and stuff, so you know, if you wait a week or two, the rules might change again."

"So there's a gray area. You can decide to let us in or not?" Griffin asked.

"There's no gray area. Everything's black or white with us."

"But we're going to be colorado residents," Griffin said.

The soldier became exasperated. "Are you *current* residents? Does *anyone* with you have a current colorado driver's license?"

"No. We're from illinois. We want to enter the state as political refugees. We want to leave the united states. We're comin' to colorado to live under No Law. Are you sayin' we're not allowed to leave the country?"

"Ok, pull over into that lane there, follow it to the parking area, and we'll figure it out. Right now!"

"Um, can we just figure it out here?" Griffin asked. "We've done nothin' to hurt anyone. We are law-abiding citizens, and we're going freely into the No Law republic of colorado. We demand safe passage."

Looking out the window, Gabe Dismas saw things become blurry. The soldiers outside became dark objects. Shapes shifted. Suddenly everything appeared to have been drawn with black crayon. The soldier at Maggie's window unhooked the narrow strap that crossed the butt of his gun. Gabe gasped. *I'm not wearing a bulletproof vest,* he thought. *Everyone is but me.* He shrunk himself down lower into the backseat, wondering if bullets could penetrate the minivan's exterior. The second soldier unholstered his weapon, and the third went quickly back into his glass booth and picked up a microphone.

An announcement came over a loudspeaker. "DRIVER. MOVE IMMEDIATELY INTO THE RIGHT LANE AND FOLLOW THE ORANGE CONES TO THE PARKING AREA. STAY IN YOUR VEHICLE WITH YOUR HANDS ON THE WHEEL UNTIL INSTRUCTED."

"Drive!" Griffin screamed. "Go, Maggie! Go!" Griffin yelled. Maggie hit the gas and the minivan tires screeched on the pavement. The vehicle lurched forward to the left, hitting the first soldier and knocking him over. His clipboard clattered to the road.

Maggie slammed on the brakes after running into the soldier and stared around, bewildered. "But they won't—"

The first soldier bounced up, and the two soldiers fell into the kneeling position almost simultaneously, guns out, gripped in right hands, left hands holding right wrists. One on each side of the solid white line. The sheets of paper on the clipboard fluttered errantly.

"Guns up! Hit the gas!" Griffin said. "Do it the way I told you! Go now! Maggie, go!"

Maggie ignored Griffin and swung open the driver's door and leaned out. "Don't shoot, please," she said, her voice sounding almost saintly. Her knuckles were white and her throat fluttered, pulsing with terror. Her open door let in the crisp smells of the autumn morning.

"Come out of the car with your hands over your head!" yelled the soldier who'd been holding the clipboard, sounding like a well-programmed machine. "You and all your passengers, ma'am. We see them."

Griffin yelled, "We aren't getting out! We demand free passage!"

The two soldiers looked at each other, and something barely perceptible passed between them. Griffin, his nerves strung up to a point where he seemed to be operating with a sixth sense, caught it. He held the phone to his mouth and yelled, "Blitz! GO! GO! GO! GO! GO! Everyone blitz!"

Griffin tromped his foot on Maggie's right shoe, his lips drawing back into panicked urgency. The minivan ripped forward, Maggie's door slammed shut at the same moment that two hollow punching noises struck it, making it rock sideways. Then the windshield blew in, splattering them with bits of glass. Maggie threw up both hands to protect her face, and Griffin leaned savagely against her, swinging the wheel to aim the careening minivan towards colorado.

"Steer!" Griffin shouted at Maggie, "Steer! Steer! *Steer!*"

Maggie's hands grabbed the wheel and turned it too sharply. The minivan swerved between the guard booths, breaking the wooden gate arm. The passenger side of the minivan scraped along the booth, shooting sparks into the air. Gabe caught a crazy glimpse of the soldiers whirling and firing at them. He picked up his assault rifle and fired through the back windshield, his whole attention on aiming and shooting his gun. Beside him, Spit had turned and was firing also.

"Aim! Watch out! Don't shoot our guys coming through!" Griffin yelled. "*Aim!* Gabe! *Mark!* Spit! Aim at the soldiers! Don't hit our guys!"

There was another hollow *thunnn!* as a bullet smashed a hole through the rear hatch. The minivan fishtailed and Maggie screamed and hung onto the wheel, whipping it to try and keep it on the interstate.

Maggie's hands turned the wheel and the vehicle finally found the road. As the guns roared inside and out, Maggie accelerated and the minivan lurched. The center rearview mirror exploded.

All Gabe heard were gunshots ringing in his ears. He saw a black flash and then blood exploded all over his hands, his chest, and his legs. Suddenly he was in so much pain that he went numb. Amidst the noise of gunfire and engines and screams, he saw his mother appear before him.

"Come with me, Mark," she said, and he followed her down a grassy path where she sat down on a wooden bench.

"You're bleeding, my darling," his mother said, taking his hands in hers. His blood smeared and dripped from their intertwined fingers into the grass. His hands felt cold, and the blood was gross and messy, but the red liquid warmed them.

"What are you doing here, Mark?"

"I'm Gabe Dismas now. I just want to live free."

"Freedom doesn't work, Mark. The government must control everything. The government must control every aspect of our lives. Our birth, our education, our relationships, our work, our health, our food, our water, and now your death."

"I don't agree with you," Gabe said.

"That is why you are dying," his mother said. "You're almost dead."

"No," Gabe said. "I will never die. I will leave this earth, but I will live forever."

Spit looked over at Gabe talking to himself, blood bubbling up through his lips while he tried to talk. He heard Gabe say, "I'm Gabe Dismas now. I just want to live free."

"Don't worry, my man!" Spit yelled. "We're going to make it! We're across the border, ok, Gabe? *Just hang in there!* Just keep your head down and hang in there. You're going to be ok!"

"I don't agree with you," Gabe said.

"Trust me, ok? You are not going to die! Just hang in there and you're going to be ok. You're not going to die, Gabe!"

"No," Gabe said. "I will never die. I will leave this earth, but I will live forever." And then a large blob of dark-purple blood shot out from Gabe's mouth and nose, and his face fell, smashing against the inside door of the minivan.

"Oh my god! I think Gabe's dead!" Spit yelled. "Gabe's dead, man!"

"Ok! Just hit the gas, Maggie! Go! Go! *GO!*" Griffin yelled. Then he yelled into his phone, "Everybody fire on your way through! Fire it up! Keep 'em all laying low!"

The line of vehicles plowed across the colorado border, passengers firing out of their side windows, guns blasting, exploding. The line of illinois plates raced forward on wobbling hunks of shot-up metal, some riding on sparking, flaming rims, but they kept their momentum and crossed through the checkpoint. The soldiers and federal border agents ducked and hid behind barricades for cover, several popping up to shoot at the line of vehicles racing past them.

Griffin's minivan mounted a small rise. On top of it, Griffin said, "Slow down, Maggie." His ears were ringing, and his head felt as if nails had been pushed into it. "We almost got wasted," he said, looking back at Spit who was wiping blood off Gabe's face.

"They almost blew us away," Spit said, exhaling in a huge huff.

Griffin stared at Gabe. At Gabe's feet, he saw blood drying on the fringes of dark-red pools. Looking back through the blown-out rear window, he saw familiar minivans following them. He looked at Maggie and yelled, "Pull over!"

Maggie pulled over quickly, clumsily, into the breakdown lane, skidding the car around in a sputtering half-turn that sprayed gravel into the air before coming to a stop.

Maggie turned to Griffin. "They tried to kill us," she said wonderingly.

"They tried to kill us."

Griffin was speaking into his phone, "Everyone keep driving on seventy-six towards denver if you're ok. Rally point in denver. We pulled over for a minute, but we're fine. Don't stop if you don't need to! Keep going if you can. Anyone who needs help right now, pull over when you see me. Is everyone ok? Is everyone through the border? Who's not ok?"

All seven minivans and one of the two u-hauls reported in. Ex and Ray reported their minivans were too shot-up to make it to denver. Across the group, two children had been shot bad and were possibly dying. Six adults had been hit and were bleeding but were being bandaged up and maybe would make it.

"Ok, Ex and Ray, coming over the first small hill, I'm on the other side waiting for you. Stop here. Fish and Columbus, you stop also. We'll move people and what stuff will fit from the shot-up vans into Fish's and Columbus's vans. Everyone else keep driving!"

A voice replied, "This is Fish. Will do. Cig and Club got nailed, Griff. The feds shot their u-haul up. They're back at the checkpoint. I hope they're gonna live. But they ain't coming with us."

Griffin looked down, closed his eyes, and said into the phone, "Ok. Ugh… Ok. Everyone else just keep going."

Ex and Ray showed up and pulled their crippled minivans into the breakdown lane. Fish and Columbus pulled over, and everyone worked to hustle passengers and supplies from the shot-up vehicles into the other two vans.

In the distance, rising and converging, came the sound of sirens.

"Oh my god! They're coming after us!" Maggie yelled.

"Yep. Let's go! That's it for equipment – leave the rest behind. We got all the passengers moved and the cash. Fish and Columbus, let's move! Get in and go! There's no time to cram more stuff. Spit, get some rifles with extra clips and get over here!"

As the screams of sirens rose louder behind them, Fish and Columbus hopped into their vans, and their two loaded-up vehicles pulled away. Spit handed Griffin an assault rifle and they leapt out of the van right as a first federal humvee pulled up behind them. They sprayed gunfire, blowing out the tires. The engine exploded and the vehicle came to a careening, sagging stop twenty yards away. They could see the humvee driver and passenger, slumped over and motionless.

When the second military cruiser came over the rise, Griffin and Spit were kneeling in the center of the interstate, their rifles held firmly at shoulder level, aimed directly at the horizon. Extra clips were between them on the road. The green-metal military vehicle was doing eighty easily, and still accelerating, some cowboy soldier at the wheel with too much engine up front and videogame visions of victory in his eyes. The driver perhaps saw Griffin and Spit, perhaps tried to stop. It didn't matter. There was no dodging the wall of armor-piercing gunfire he accelerated into. The windshield shattered and the tires exploded as if there had been dynamite inside. The vehicle took off like a drunken bird, gunning across the shoulder in howling, uncontrolled flight. It crashed nose-first, less than a hundred yards away. The driver rammed through the windshield like a torpedo and slammed into the ground.

A third vehicle came almost as fast, and it took Griffin and Spit even less time to find the tires. It slid around in a smoking half-turn and rolled over three times, spraying glass and metal, smashing the cabin flat. It finally came to a wobbling, smoking rest a hundred feet from them.

Griffin stood up, looked down, and saw the spent brass bullet casings gleaming in the morning sun. He listened closely. It was quiet. The sirens had stopped. He looked toward the minivan and then the second cruiser exploded, spewing shrapnel above and around them. Griffin was knocked flat to the ground by the blast. He felt white-hot pain and then his side suddenly began to throb in pulsing, aching cycles.

He saw Spit run towards the minivan and got up to follow him, hopping clumsily, gun held firm in his left hand. He lost his balance and fell hard, scraping both knees. He got up again and stumbled forward.

When he finally got to the minivan, Spit was in the backseat, panting. Maggie was in the driver's seat, staring out, transfixed by the burning military vehicles. Griffin slid into the car, breathing hard. The world insisted on going in and out. Warped sounds angled through his brain.

When Griffin got in, Maggie shrank from him. "What happened to the cops?" she asked.

"I killed them."

"You killed them. You killed those men."

Griffin didn't reply. He just slid down in the passenger seat, waiting to hear more sirens, looking at the horizon for more vehicles cresting the hill. There was nothing. Just stillness.

"They killed Gabe. They wanted to kill me. You. Us," Griffin said. "Drive. Fast."

Maggie sat still, looking out.

"Drive!" Griffin yelled.

"This is madness. We're all going to be killed," Maggie said, her voice trembling.

"Drive," Griffin mumbled. "Just drive."

Maggie pulled onto the road. Griffin saw blood smeared all over the green blouse she wore over her armored vest. *Whose blood?* Griffin wondered but didn't ask.

Maggie gripped the steering wheel and stared straight ahead. She drove. No one spoke. As the minivan raced southwest down the interstate, Griffin looked at the plastic dashboard and studied the small bumps and dimples in its texture. *We got farther than we had any right to,* Griffin thought. *We're across the border. We're free, in colorado, in No Law. We're in a new world now. I'm a million miles from that chicago front porch where I asked Maggie to come here.* His eyes looked in the side mirror, searching, but there were no green-metal vehicles behind them, no blue lights. They continued on towards denver.

Sometime later the denver skyline and the rocky mountains appeared on the horizon. Griffin stared, dazed, catching glints of late morning light reflecting off the snow-covered peaks. Their magnificence amazed him. He'd never seen a world like this. It was as if children had made this world, with all freedom and nature and no evil. The sun on the snow-capped mountains was a middle finger from god to anyone who ever tried to control anyone else.

Everywhere he looked, things seemed wilder, brighter, more welcoming, like all this time he'd been seeing the world through dark glasses, and he'd never realized what everything really looked like.

And now he was seeing it all for the first time.

EPILOGUE
anamnesis

In southwest colorado, a ranch spreads across hundreds of acres. At the eastern edge of the property, a stream runs deep and green. The water is warm, for it has already ambled for hours through the afternoon sun. The stream is lined with trees – aspens, willows, cottonwoods, boxelders, and pines. On a sandy bank under the trees, the leaves lie so crisp that they break when mice or men ruffle through them. The ground is covered with the tracks of foxes, prairie dogs, and deer that come to drink.

A dirt path runs through the aspens and among the pines, a path beaten hard by boys, girls, men, and women coming down from the ranch, in groups and alone, to swim, or to fish, or to just sit and think. In front of the large fallen trunk of a giant cottonwood is an ash pile made by many fires, embers are still smoking, remnants of recent flames, and a limb is worn smooth by people sitting together and alone, staring at the interwoven mysteries and answers that flicker warmly within the pyre.

On the banks, some rabbits sit quietly, like small brown statues. And then from the direction of the path comes the sound of footsteps on leaves. The rabbits hurry noiselessly into the brush, close to their secret burrows. A bobcat pads away from the water. A golden eagle ascends into the air and glides downriver. For a moment the place becomes lifeless, and then two men emerge from the path and come into the opening by a green pool.

Two men stand by the stream and look into the twists and turns of ghostlike smoke rising into the air. The man named Spit said, "Griff, we're in heaven. Chicago was our life before we died and came here. Everythin' you said came true. You told us how it would be, and you were right."

Griffin Turner replied, "We did it together."

"You got us here."

"We all got it goin'. A house and a farm, cows and some pigs. The windmill is workin' great. Now we got the chicken run and the pig pen. The orchard's got apples, blackberries, raspberries, pears, and pumpkins."

"We're livin' off the fat of the land, my brother," Spit said.

"That fresh milk from the cows… the cream is so thick you got to cut it with a knife and take it out with a spoon."

"Fresh churned butter. That's the fat of the land I like," Spit laughed. "I've never ate so good in my life. Never worked so hard either," he laughed again. "That smokehouse smoking the bacon and the hams, and makin' sausage an' all like that. And we caught over a hundred trout running up river and salted 'em and smoked 'em. Ain't nothing so nice as smoked trout for breakfast. When the fruit comes in, we'll can it – and tomatoes – they're easy to can."

"It's a lot of work."

"It's *hard* work, but it ain't like we're working *long*. Maybe six, seven hours a day. It's not like working fast-food sixteen hours a day to still be broke – it's all *ours*. We put the seeds in the ground, and we take the crop up. It's all us. We reap what we sow."

"You sound more and more like a farmer," Griffin laughed.

"We belong here. We've always belonged here. There's no more runnin' round. No more street corners, drugs, cops, no more handouts. We have our own place where we belong."

The two men stood there, still. The curls of smoke twisted and turned into haunting shapes, spirits floating in the shadows of the sunset.

The sun was leaving and shade stole over the water. An easy rush of wind sounded through the trees, sounding like ghosts of old. The aspen leaves turned up. The brown, dry leaves on the ground skittered a few feet, and rows of small wind waves flowed across the water's surface.

The two men stood there, still. They listened to the ghosts yell and laugh.

As quickly as it had come, the wind died, and all was quiet. The sun lowered, moving out of the valley, and as it went, the mountaintops blazed. Only the topmost ridges were in the sun now. The shadows in the valley were shifting, blue and soft.

The two men stood there, still. They looked at the shadows.

Sometimes, shapes inside the shadows looked like indian warriors preparing for battle.

Sometimes the shadow shapes looked like children playing.

The two men stood there, still.

They looked, and they smiled, and tears of joy glistened in their eyes.

the pause

POSTSCRIPT

Walt Whitman's caution

39—

Walt Whitman's Caution.

To The States, or any one of
    them, or any city of The
    States, Resist much, Obey
little,
Once unquestioning obedience,
    once fully enslaved,
Once fully enslaved, no nation
    race, city, of this earth,
    ever afterward resumes
    its liberty.—

ABOUT THE AUTHOR

Benjamin L. Owen resides mostly in new england with his wife, his poodle, and the intermittent ghost of his dead cat. His favorite authors include George Orwell and J.D. Salinger. *Last Way West* is his second novel.

benl.owen@yahoo.com

Made in the USA
San Bernardino, CA
26 November 2017